Troubled Waters

To Mary —
Hope you enjoy the book!

Best wishes,
Donna J. Ferguson

Mickey Sutter mystery series, Volume 1

Troubled Waters

D.J. Ferguson

Writer's Showcase
San Jose New York Lincoln Shanghai

Troubled Waters

Writer's Showcase
an imprint of iUniverse.com, Inc.

For information address:
iUniverse.com, Inc.
5220 S 16th, Ste. 200
Lincoln, NE 68512
www.iuniverse.com

ISBN: 0-595-16000-X

Printed in the United States of America

For Peter M. Sutter who knew how to live life to its fullest.

I would like to thank my family and friends for their support and encouragement. And special thanks to Barry Fanning for his harsh criticism, hours of editing, and bulldog insistence that I get it right.

Chapter *One*

*M*ickey silently cursed the plunging waves and wondered for the umpteenth time what the hell she'd gotten herself into. The sky was a solid mass of dark gray clouds, and a light drizzling rain blurred the horizon. Scanning the water ahead, she clenched the wheel of the thirty-two-foot vessel with a white-knuckled grip. The straits were littered with branches, logs and hunks of wood drifting along in the current, and a stiff westerly breeze had whipped the sea into white-caps, making it hard to spot debris on the rough surface. Some of that elusive Washington sunshine would help, but she might as well hope to win the lottery.

It would also help if her nephew would sit up and pay attention. She had arranged for someone to drive her pickup out west, so she wouldn't have to make the trip alone. It was nice to have an extra set of eyes on board, especially in weather like this. So much for that plan. With his head against the wall and eyes closed, Colin was sound asleep. Mickey thought about waking him, but decided he wouldn't be much help any-way. Colin could hardly see past the bow of the boat and refused to wear glasses—said it scared away the girls. So why the hell doesn't he wear contact lenses?

Mickey shook her head in annoyance and squirmed in her seat, numb from two-and-a-half hours of sitting. Her eyes burned from straining to see into the dark water below the foaming crests of oncom-ing waves. After staring so long, her mind had begun playing tricks on her, imagining things that weren't really there. She rubbed a hand over her face and exhaled loudly.

Moving along at twenty knots, *Perseverance* carved a path through the choppy seas, seemingly unaffected by the weather. Below the surface, the boat's twin propellers churned the water with horsepower to spare, sending sheets of spray out both sides of the V-shaped hull. Mickey knew the boat could handle the conditions just fine—it was herself she was worried about. She glanced at the gauges for the engines, then checked the loran to make sure she was still on course. Returning her gaze to the water ahead, she saw a long, dark shape appear in front of the boat.

"Oh shit!" Mickey cranked the wheel hard to the left, pulling as fast as she could. She caught another glimpse of the partially submerged log as it disappeared under a wave. Jerking the wheel back the other way, she tried to swing the stern away from the log. Seconds later, she heard the thud of wood hitting fiberglass and grabbed the throttles to pull them back. The boat slowed with a sudden lurch, and Colin jerked upright in his seat. Mickey heard a second thump and knew the log had connected with the outdrives.

"What the hell was that?" Colin blurted out, wide awake now.

"Son-of-a-bitch," Mickey shouted, furious at herself for not paying more attention. "I just hit a damned log. Of all the stupid…"

"How bad is it? I mean, did it damage anything?"

"How the hell should I know? Maybe if you'd been awake…" Mickey stopped herself, regretting the outburst. "I just can't see anything in this lousy weather."

She slumped in her seat for a moment, wishing it were Pete sitting in this chair instead of herself. She never wanted to be the captain. God, if she could just go back in time and change the clock by a few minutes, he would have been somewhere else when that damned drunk ran the red light.

"No, you're right," Colin said, interrupting her thoughts. "I should've been watching. Maybe I would've seen something." He swore softly under his breath and ran his fingers through his closely-cropped hair, just starting to grow out since his discharge from the Marine Corps a few weeks ago.

The boat drifted with a sloppy rocking motion, pushed along by wind and waves. Testing the damage, Mickey shifted into gear and gave it a little throttle. A tremendous vibration shook the vessel, and she immediately shifted back into neutral. With a heavy sigh, she turned to Colin.

"Hey, forget it. Right now, we need to raise the outdrives and see what we're up against. Go back and watch to make sure they come up together, okay?" Mickey didn't want to bend the steering bar between the two drive units. She'd done enough damage already.

Colin looked concerned, but said nothing as he slid open the door of the cabin, letting in a burst of cold air. A large wave splashed against the side of the boat, covering the deck with spray, and he paused to grab his jacket before stepping outside. The boat tossed wildly, and Colin lurched unsteadily as he made his way to the stern. Reaching the engine room, with only a six-inch cap rail between him and the ocean, he resorted to crawling.

Mickey waited until he clambered over the dive hoses and kneeled at the transom, then pushed the buttons on the trim control to raise the outdrives.

"Looking good," Colin yelled, giving her a thumbs up. He watched for a minute longer, then waved his arm and whistled for her to stop.

Mickey shut down the engines and went outside to have a look. The starboard propeller had taken a beating. All three blades were bent, and one had a huge crack in the aluminum, all the way down to the hub. Well, that one's going to the scrap heap. Kiss five hundred bucks good-bye. Still, she should be thankful that the damage wasn't worse. If she'd hit the log with the outdrives turned sideways, it would have busted them clean off. Then she'd be worried about sinking, instead of pondering how to get the hell out of here.

Mickey considered the options. They were five miles offshore, smack in the middle of the shipping lanes, and Port Angeles harbor was about fifteen miles behind them. Running on one engine, the trip would take close to two hours and they'd run out of daylight long before getting there. As much as she hated the idea, she'd rather change the prop right here and get under way. If they could make it to Sekiu before nightfall, they'd anchor up and go on in the morning.

Her mind made up, she turned to Colin. "The spare props are in the engine room. If you'll drag the hoses out of the way, I know exactly where they're at."

"The hoses are no problem. I can lift this," he said, grabbing the handle on the front of the engine room. The hatch cover was heavy, and two coils of diving hose added at least a hundred pounds, but Colin raised the lid easily. Mickey was impressed at how strong he'd become. This was not the same skinny kid who'd gone off to join the service four years ago.

Colin braced the hatch cover against his knee while Mickey climbed inside and worked her way down beside the starboard engine. Rocked by waves, the boat took a sudden lurch, and Mickey fell against the hot exhaust manifold, burning her wrist. Too busy to notice the pain, she worked to uncover the props and pick out the one with left-handed pitch. By the time Mickey got herself turned around and set the propeller out on deck, Colin was gritting his teeth.

"Some time today," he said, only half-kidding. "This is getting heavy."

"You try squeezing in there next time," she retorted. Being the smallest person on board, Mickey always got stuck with the jobs that required squeezing into tight places. It was not her idea of fun.

A large wave smacked loudly against the transom, and Mickey turned to stare at the raised outdrives. The boat pitched and rolled erratically, and every third or fourth wave washed clear over the propellers. Changing a prop in rough water wasn't her idea of fun either, but someone had to do it.

"I better put on my rain gear," she said without enthusiasm. "This is gonna be a wet job."

"You want me to do it?" Colin offered, not sounding too eager.

Mickey wasn't sure she was ready to trust him with this kind of job. He had never changed a prop before, and Colin wasn't what she'd call mechanically inclined.

"No, I'll go. Just get me the channel locks and big screwdriver from the toolbox, and grab that piece of two-by-four out of the crate," she said, ducking into the cabin to put on her gear. When she came back out, Colin was sitting on the engine cover, tools in hand.

Kneeling down at the transom, Mickey paused, trying to bolster her courage. It was an awkward job because she had to climb out on the outdrive facing the water, and there was really nothing to hang onto. Mickey had done it before—inside the harbor where it was flat calm— but never in rough water like this. She was secretly tempted to let Colin try it, but that wouldn't be right. Pete would never have asked someone else to do a dangerous job for him. Damn, she wished he was here to do it now.

"You sure you don't want me to do this?" Colin asked again.

"Yeah, I'm sure," she said, not being entirely truthful. She wasn't sure at all, but it wouldn't do any good to admit it. "I'll get into position, and you can pass me the tools. Just make damn sure you're ready to grab me if I start to fall."

Tightly gripping the handrail on the stern of the boat, Mickey cautiously placed first one foot on the outdrive, then the other. Letting out a deep breath, she whispered a silent prayer to Pete. "Hey mister— wherever you are—I need your help on this one."

Still clinging to the rail behind her, she sank to her knees, letting them rest against the metal housing. A wave splashed over the outdrive, covering her boots, and Mickey fought the urge to panic. As the water receded, she tried turning loose of the rail. The boat suddenly pitched into a steep wave, and one of her knees slipped off the outdrive. Mickey quickly grabbed the handrail, cursing loudly.

This was no damn good. Her feet were too close together to give her any stability. She needed to straddle the drive unit. Moving carefully, she slid her feet down the sides until they rested against something solid, then kneeled on the knobby ends of the hydraulic rams. Her legs were pressed against the housing like vise grips and it was uncomfortable as hell, but at least she felt more stable. Mickey took a deep breath and let go of the rail. The next wave washed clear over her lap, but this time she stayed put.

"Okay," she said, letting out a tense breath. "Let's get this over with."

She slid the tip of the screwdriver under a metal tab on the star washer and pried upward. The forty-two-degree water felt icy cold on her hands, making her fingers clumsy with numbness. Taking the two-by-four from Colin, she wedged it against the prop to keep it from turning, then reached back for the channel locks. The large brass nut turned easily, and Mickey silently thanked Pete for greasing the threads. She passed the wrench back to Colin and used both hands to catch the washer and nut.

"Whatever you do, don't drop them," she cautioned as he took them from her.

"You don't need to remind me," he said with a touch of irritation.

"Yeah, I know. But if we lose anything, we're up shit creek."

Dreading the next part, Mickey leaned forward, grasped the propeller and pulled upward. It didn't budge. She straightened for a minute and moaned with frustration. Her legs were cramped with pain, and wet strands of shoulder-length hair clung to her face. Ready to try again, she grabbed hold of the prop and pulled as hard as she could. Just as she was about to give up, it started to move and she breathed a sigh of relief.

"You ready to take this?" Mickey asked, holding the mangled propeller. She knew he was, but she needed to say it. Too much nervous energy made her talkative. The boat took a violent dip as she handed it over, and Mickey clamped her legs together even tighter around the housing. She wanted this to be over with. Taking the new prop from Colin, she slid it onto the shaft and reached back for the washer and nut. Stiff and numb with cold, she could barely move her fingers. After fumbling for a minute, she was able to get the nut started, and Colin handed her the channel locks. As she adjusted the pliers to fit the nut, they slipped out of her hand and bounced off the outdrive, making a little splash before disappearing into the dark water below.

"Noooo…" Mickey shouted with frustration. "And here I was telling you to be careful. I can't believe it."

"Don't worry about it. Tools are expendable. Just hang on tight while I get you a crescent wrench," Colin said, jumping to his feet.

Waiting for him to return, she clung to the outdrive and felt her eyes fill with tears. What the hell was she doing out here? Trying to prove to the world she could do a man's job?

"Just don't drop this one," Colin teased gently as he passed her the wrench. "Or we'll be swimming home."

"Real funny, smart ass," Mickey replied, but she did manage a smile. Clenching the wrench with an iron grip, she tightened the nut, then hammered down the tabs on the star washer to lock it in place. God, what a relief. Now if she could just get herself back on the boat.

"I don't think my legs will work," she said, reaching back for the handrail.

"Just lean toward me," Colin said. "I'll get you." Slipping his arms under her shoulders, he lifted her backwards onto the boat as though her hundred and twenty pounds weighed nothing.

It felt so good to be back on solid turf, Mickey laughed loudly as she flopped down on the engine cover. The numbness in her legs soon began to wear off, making them tingle painfully, and she rubbed them through her jeans while Colin put the tools away. A few minutes later she forced herself to move.

"Let's get the hell out of here."

CHAPTER *Two*

$\mathcal{W}$ith the benefit of hindsight, Mickey realized that it had been incredibly stupid to leave Port Townsend so late in the day. Even without the prop-changing fiasco, there was no way they could have made it to Neah Bay before nightfall. It was bad enough dodging driftwood and logs during the day, but trying to do it after dark would be an absolute nightmare. Dammit-all-to-hell, why didn't she think things through, instead of acting on impulse? She couldn't afford to make mistakes now that she was captain.

The sensible thing would have been to leave the following morning. They weren't in that big a hurry. The season didn't open until Monday, and this was only Saturday. But she had been impatient, wanting to get there early so they could rest up for the first day of diving. Mickey had picked sea urchins for ten of her thirty-five years, and she was pretty tough. But the first day underwater was always brutal, and there was no way to get in shape for it, except doing it.

She glanced at the gauges, hating to take her eyes off the water for even an instant. The visibility was getting worse, and Mickey was afraid she might hit something else.

"How you doing?" Colin asked, noticing her worried expression.

"I don't know if I'm cut out for this job," she said, shaking her head. "Pete always seemed so calm in situations like this. I don't know how the hell he did it."

"I bet there were plenty of times he wanted to be somewhere else."

"Well, you wouldn't have known by looking at him. He was so cool about everything." Mickey smiled sadly, then blinked to force back the tears. "I'd give anything to have him back," she added, her voice thick with emotion.

It was hard to believe it had only been four months since Pete was killed by that drunk driver. Four months since her life had been turned upside down. Four months since she'd lost her best friend and husband of fifteen years. Mickey was now the sole owner of their commercial diving boat, a huge responsibility. She didn't admit it to many people, but it scared the hell out of her.

Colin stared out the window, not sure what to say. Mickey had done a great job of pulling herself together after Pete's death, but today she seemed to be unraveling. "Hey Mickey, there isn't anybody who can fill Pete's shoes, but you'll make a damn good captain. You've got the experience and enough guts to pull it off."

"Thanks for saying it, but I'm not sure I believe you."

"I'm not just saying that to make you feel better," he said, getting frustrated. "You just need to make up your mind that you want to be here. Nobody is making you do this. You could hire someone to run the boat and make a few bucks off the boat's share." Squinting his eyes, he looked directly at her. "You could probably get a job bookkeeping or something. Forget this crazy business."

"I'm not a quitter."

"I didn't say you were. But if this isn't what you want to be doing—if it isn't fun anymore—then screw it. Do something else. Find something that will make you happy."

"But I don't want to do anything else," Mickey insisted. "This is my life."

"Then get a grip. Having to change a prop out here really sucked, but you did it. The boat's still in one piece, and no one got hurt. Think what a great story you'll have to tell over a few beers." Colin smiled and looked out the front window at the parade of whitecaps tumbling toward the boat. They seemed to go on forever, blending together in a blur of white. "Don't be so hard on yourself. Anybody could miss seeing a log in this crap. If you want to blame someone, blame me. I was the one sleeping on the job." Hopping down from his seat, he added, "The only thing I can see–is my way to the cookies."

"You haven't earned any cookies," she protested.

Colin gave her one of his boyish grins. With his red hair and fair skin dotted with freckles, he looked younger than twenty-four. Disappearing into the lower cabin, he returned with a round cookie tin and pried the lid off. Seeing that they were oatmeal and raisin, his favorite, he smiled and grabbed a handful. At five-foot-eight, Colin was not very big, but his size was deceiving. A wide set of shoulders and hard muscles were hidden beneath the loose workshirt, the result of four years pumping iron as a Marine. Still chewing, he reached for more.

Mickey saw him go for another handful and shouted to get his attention, "Hey! You plan to eat them all, or do I get a few?"

"I thought maybe you were on a diet or something."

"Pass 'em over, you little rat, and don't forget who's in charge of your air supply while you're underwater."

Grinning, he leaned over with the tin of cookies, and Mickey grabbed three while she had the chance. With as much exercise as she got, dieting was not even part of her vocabulary. Feeling better after Colin's words of encouragement, Mickey was suddenly in the mood to talk.

"Did I ever tell you how I met your uncle?" she asked. Colin shook his head, and she continued, "He was working at a dive shop in Walnut Creek, and I came in to get some equipment repaired. The first thing he did was insult me–said my gear was junk, and then suggested I take his diving class. Learn to do it the right way! I got huffy and told him I'd been diving since I was fourteen and planned to become a commercial diver. You know what he did? He laughed at me! Arrogant asshole." She smiled at the memory, easing the frown lines on her face.

Colin chuckled. "And you went out with him after that?"

"Not right away. A couple of months later, I signed up to go abalone diving. Turned out to be a nasty day, cold wind out of the north, big swells rolling in. Most of the divers decided to stay out of the water, but I was too macho to chicken out. I'd never been snorkeling in rough water before, and the truth is—I was scared shitless. I didn't get any abs that day, just clung to the float while Pete plucked them off the rocks. Then it was a long swim back to the beach fighting a current, and I couldn't keep up. Pete told me to hang on to the float, and he pretty much towed me back to shore. Talk about a humbling experience."

Colin smiled and said, "I bet he didn't miss a chance to rub it in either."

"No. He never mentioned it. Back on the beach, he told everyone what a trooper I was, and we started dating soon after that and went diving nearly every weekend. The funny thing is, it was Pete who got me started picking sea urchins. Now I'm hooked on it, and there's no way I'm quitting."

"You sounded ready to a little while ago," he said in a smart-ass tone of voice.

"Hey, just because I bitch about something, doesn't mean I'm ready to throw in the towel. It's just my way of letting off steam."

"Good. I'd hate to think this was my last batch of homemade cookies."

Mickey shot him a dirty look before smiling at his joke.

"By the way, when is Rick bringing *Rough Rider* out?" Colin asked.

"Tomorrow morning. He still had some work to do." Rick had hinted that they could make the run together if she'd wait for him, and right now, she wished she had. The ocean could be a lonely place when things got ugly.

"What about George?"

"Coming from Anacortes, he might be on his way already. I'll try an' raise him on the radio," she said, reaching for the mike. George Kessler was one of her favorites among the crew of sea urchin divers, and she looked forward to seeing him. He always seemed so cheerful, even when things went wrong, and she hoped that some of his optimism would rub off on her. Mickey gave a call for the *Sheri-Lynn* and was pleasantly surprised to hear George's voice come booming back.

"Good to hear you, Mickey. Where you at—over?"

"Half a mile from Pillar Point. Colin's on board eating all the cookies, and he says hi. What's your location?"

"Just leaving the San Juans. I'm off the south end of Lopez. Should be able to spot the lighthouse, but the visibility sucks and I can't see a thing—over."

"Tell me about it. I hit a log and had to change the prop out here. I'm hoping to make Sekiu before dark and go the rest of the way in the morning. We've got extra food if you want to join us for dinner–over."

"Thanks for the offer, but you forget how slow this beast is. At twelve knots it would be a midnight snack by the time I got there. I better keep chugging—over."

"Yeah, I hear ya. Just don't get run over by a freighter. That could ruin your whole day."

"Not to worry, Mickey. I'll keep a close eye on the radar. Say, have you heard anything about the price?"

"Not much. None of the local buyers would quote me a price, so I called the guy we sell to when we're down south. He said they paid a buck-twenty-five last week, but there's hardly any urchins coming in. They're getting hammered by one storm after another–over."

"Well, that's good news for us. The market must be hot right now. When the price is over a dollar, it sure helps get me motivated—especially in weather like this–over."

Talk of a high price got Colin's attention. He had worked with Mickey and Pete before going into the service, back when the price was a measly twenty-five cents a pound. He leaned forward in his seat and flashed Mickey a thumbs-up.

His eagerness was contagious, and Mickey smiled. "Colin's ready to suit up so he can be the first one in the water," she replied, laughing, then added, "Do you have any idea who you're going to sell to?"

"I'd like to sell to the guy who's paying a buck-twenty-five. Any chance of him sending a truck up from California?"

"I didn't ask, but I think if we had enough boats lined up, he might be interested. Let's talk some more when we get out there. I sure don't like any of the local buyers. There isn't an honest one in the bunch—over."

"You got that right. Guess for starters, I'll just bring in my load and sell to the highest bidder. Well, it was good talking with you, Mickey," George said, wrapping it up. "Have a safe trip and I'll see you out there. Stop by for coffee in the morning."

"We'll do that. Are you sure you want to go all the way tonight? Be awful late by the time you get in, won't it?"

"Yeah, after midnight sometime. But I hired a guy to tend for me, and he's meeting me with my truck. He'll be sleeping in the cab if I don't show—over."

"O.K. George. Take care and we'll see you tomorrow. This is *Perseverance*. I'll be clear."

"See you later, Mickey. Tell Colin he better save me a couple cookies. *Sheri-Lynn*, clear."

Smiling sheepishly, Colin put the lid back on the cookies and turned to look out the window. The sky was noticeably darker, and he could just barely make out the shoreline. "How far to Sekiu?" he asked.

"A few miles."

"Still planning to stop?"

"Shit yes," she said, irritated at the question. "George doesn't mind running at night because he goes slow. He hits a log, it just bounces off. You've seen what can happen to us." Mickey glared at him for a second, as though daring him to challenge her decision.

Colin shrugged and settled back against the seat cushion. He was getting used to her sudden mood swings.

Mickey stared ahead into the growing darkness, the white foam of cresting waves barely discernable against a deep pool of black. Spotting the beacon light on Slip Point less than a mile away, she breathed a sigh of relief. In ten minutes they'd be safely anchored, and she could finally relax–at least for tonight.

CHAPTER *Three*

Stretching his arms over his head, George Kessler surrendered to a huge yawn. His eyes filled with tears, and he lifted the gold-rimmed glasses from his nose to wipe them away. With his elbows braced against the wheel, he rested his head in his hands and closed his eyes. God, that felt good.

After a few seconds, his breathing deepened and he started to nod off. As his arm slipped from the wheel, he jerked upright, shaking his head. Dammit, he couldn't let himself do that. He had to stay awake. Sliding open a side window, he sucked in a breath of cold air that smelled of salt and seaweed, the scent of beach at low tide.

George glanced at the dim glow of the radar screen, then checked the loran to be sure he was still on course. A thick fog had moved in, wrapping the boat in heavy white mist. He couldn't see the waves, but he could feel them as the thirty-four-foot vessel climbed slowly up the face of an oncoming wave, then picked up speed as she slid down the backside. Motoring west, the waves had gotten bigger, long ocean swells rolling in from the Pacific, and he hoped they calmed down before opening day.

Monday morning a fleet of fifty-some diving boats would anchor in kelp beds along the rocky coast, searching for carpets of spiny red sea urchins. To conserve the resource, they were limited to one diver in the water at a time and allowed to work only three days a week. George shook his head in disgust. What they should've done was limit the number of licenses five years ago when there weren't so many boats.

D.J. Ferguson

He still made a pretty good living, but it got harder every year, picking urchins by hand and stuffing them into mesh bags. Back at the dock, the urchins were sold and taken to a processing plant where workers cracked open the shells to get at the roe. The golden strips of tiny yellow eggs were then placed on wooden trays and flown direct to Japan to be served in sushi bars throughout the country. Considered a delicacy, the best roe went for as much as three-hundred-and-fifty dollars a pound.

Somebody was getting rich off sea urchins, but it sure as hell wasn't the divers. Christ, if they were paid even a tenth of what it sold for in Japan, he could afford to take his wife on that trip he'd been promising. George had always wanted to visit Japan, and he imagined taking Sheri to a high-class sushi bar in Tokyo, trying the different foods and sipping warm sake. It would be expensive, but they were long overdue for a vacation.

For the last two years, every dime he'd made had gone to pay for the new boat, but Sheri was a good sport about it. She knew how unpredictable the business was. It was a damned good thing she had her teaching job, because there were times when they had to live off her paycheck. George smiled, thinking how some of the other guys complained about their wives. He knew how lucky he was.

Close now, the harbor entrance at Neah Bay, part of the Makah Indian Reservation, stood out clearly on his radar screen. A bold green line showed the man-made breakwater stretching from Waada Island to shore, sheltering the harbor from the north. The coastline angled northwest for another seven miles, to the battered cliffs of Cape Flattery, and from there, turned abruptly southward.

The area surrounding Neah Bay was open for harvest every third year, and this would be George's fourth season here. He wondered if the place had changed at all since his last visit. It always seemed the same, like it was suspended in time. George wished he could say the same about himself, but after celebrating his thirty-eighth birthday and struggling with financial pressures for the last two years, he was feeling a lot older.

In the sheltered water of the bay, the *Sheri Lynn* surged ahead and George leaned out the window to see if he could spot Waada Island to his right, but it was lost in the mist and darkness. He had told Carl to meet him at the pier around midnight, and it was already forty minutes past. By now, Carl might have given up and fallen asleep in the truck. George decided he'd make one pass by the pier, and if he didn't spot Carl, he'd go anchor up and find him in the morning.

Pulling alongside Ocean Fish Pier, he eased the throttle off and felt the boat settle deeper in the water as it slowed. The fog was sparse near shore, and he could see the dock in the dim glow of an overhead light, but the parking area was hidden by darkness. There was no sign of life, and after a couple of minutes he gave up, shifted into gear and headed for the far end of the bay. Shallow and well-protected, it was usually the calmest place to anchor.

Ahead in the distance, George spotted the eerie glow of a light and studied his radar, trying to decide where it was coming from. The only thing at this end of the bay was the old fuel dock, but they hadn't pumped fuel there for years. The whole structure, including the barn-shaped packing plant, was slowly falling apart. His radar showed the bright green blip of a boat alongside the dock, and he couldn't imagine what it was doing there.

Changing course slightly, George brought *Sheri-Lynn* abreast of the dock, shifted into neutral and slid open his window. Grabbing his binoculars, he focused on the dock, and his mouth dropped open in shock. Tied beneath the hoist was a boat, its deck stacked high with sea urchins. George watched in stunned silence as the tender hooked two bags from the top of the pile, then signaled the hoist operator to take them up. He took a deep breath and let it out slowly, his face hot with anger.

D.J. Ferguson

"Dirty bastards," he whispered fiercely, shaking his head. George recognized the boat as the *Intruder,* owned by the Drake brothers. They were notorious poachers, and he couldn't let them get away with this. But how the hell was he going to stop them? There were probably three guys on the boat and at least one more on the dock. He was mad enough to take on all of them, but knew that was foolish. As the *Sheri-Lynn* drifted in darkness off the end of the pier, George struggled to calm himself and think it through. He suddenly remembered his running lights and switched them off.

George realized he needed to call Fisheries Enforcement. It would take them awhile to finish unloading the urchins, hopefully enough time for a fish cop to get here. He thought about using the VHF to call, but decided it was too risky, since they could be listening on a scanner. He would have to go ashore and use the land line, and the closest phone he knew of was outside a little bait-n-tackle shop near the head of the dock. George wondered if he should chance it. With *Intruder* tied to the west side of the pier, out near the end, his boat should be hidden from view by the packing plant if he snuck in on the east side. Making his decision, George eased *Sheri-Lynn* into gear, the back of his neck tingling with apprehension.

*　　*　　*　　*　　*

At the end of the pier, a man stood in the shadows, taking a leak off the edge of the dock. As he turned to leave, something caught his eye—a brief flash of red. The man stopped and stared at the blackness of the bay. He saw nothing and told himself he'd probably imagined it. Just then, the electric winch fell silent, and he heard the quiet rumble of a boat engine in the distance. Maybe it was a fishing boat looking to anchor up for the night. He stood still, trying to track its movement, and noted with alarm that it seemed to be coming closer. Stepping carefully around the empty fish totes, piles of netting and broken pallets, the man moved down the side of the dock for a better look.

* * * * *

The *Sheri-Lynn* coasted gently toward the wooden pilings, and George stepped outside to get a line on the dock. Tying a second line at the stern, he was startled by the sound of footsteps. He looked up and saw a dark figure climbing down the ladder. Reaching the bottom, the man dropped to the deck and turned toward George.

"Listen, before you say anything—I know what you're thinking…"

George cut him off, his voice full of contempt. "You asshole. Thought you'd pull a fast one, didn't you? This is bullshit."

"Wait a minute! Let's talk this over," the man said urgently.

"There's nothing to talk about," George said, towering over him menacingly. "Creeps like you belong in jail!"

"Please, hear me out. We can make a deal. Name your price. It will be the easiest money you ever make. Forget you saw anything here tonight, and you walk away with a pocket full of cash."

Clenching his fists, George took a step forward. "Get the hell off my boat, you son-of-a-bitch!"

The man opened his mouth to argue, but quickly changed his mind when he saw the look on George's face. Panic-stricken, he grabbed the ladder and began climbing.

George didn't bother chasing him. He'd be easy enough to find later. Stepping back inside the cabin, he grabbed his wallet and thumbed through the wad of business cards, looking for the one from Brad Sanders, the local fish cop. Finding it, he slipped the card into a pocket, grabbed the key from the ignition and shut the door on his way out. While climbing the ladder, George realized he'd blown it. He should have kept his cool and pretended to take the bribe. That would've bought him some time. Too late now.

Reaching the top of the ladder, George sensed movement from above and looked up. He saw something coming at him in a blur of motion and tried to duck, but it happened too fast. The board caught him solidly on the side of the head, and his glasses went flying, making a tiny splash in the water next to the boat. Stunned by the blow, his hands slipped from the ladder and with his arms flailing wildly, he fell backwards ten feet to the deck. A loud, hollow sound echoed throughout the boat when he hit.

The man stood at the top of the ladder, looking down at the dark shape of George's body, lying motionless on the deck. He listened for a moment, half expecting to hear him moaning—but there was nothing–just the raspy sound of his own breathing. His heart was pounding so hard, it felt as though it would burst out of his chest. He suddenly realized that the board was still clenched in his hands, and he heaved it as far as he could out over the water.

His legs began to shake, and he sank to his knees to keep from falling. What the hell had he done? The man forced himself to take deep breaths and think about what he should do next. He needed to come up with a plan. But first, he had to make sure George was dead.

The man stepped onto the boat, the pounding of his heart echoing in his ears. Crouching down, he placed a hand against George's neck to check for a pulse and flinched at the warm feel of the skin. Forcing his hand back down, he felt no pulse and sighed with relief. Now, if he could just make it look like an accident.

Studying the deck of the boat, he spotted the fishhold. That might work. Open the hatch, dump George in, and hopefully they'd think he fell. But he wasn't sure he could pull it off. George was big and wouldn't be easy to move.

"Come on!" he hissed under his breath, talking to himself. "Do it and get the hell out of here. You don't have all night."

Moving quickly, the man lifted the bulky hatch cover to expose the large fishhold below deck, then hooked both arms under George's armpits and dragged him to the opening. Adrenaline fueled his strength, making it seem easy. At the edge of the hold, he shoved George's legs over the side and rolled him in, wincing as the body hit bottom with a dull thud.

Anxious to be done, the man untied the stern dock line, leaving it heaped on deck. With a single line at the ladder holding the boat to the pier, he raised his hand, trying to gauge the direction of the wind, and felt a strong breeze coming from shore, blowing steadily toward the far side of the bay. Casting loose the remaining dock line, he climbed onto the ladder and pushed against the side of the boat with his feet. The heavy vessel resisted at first, hardly moving at all. Finally, the boat started to drift away from the dock and was caught by the wind. Picking up speed, *Sheri-Lynn* soon disappeared into the blackness of the night.

CHAPTER *Four*

*U*p before the sun, Mickey stepped out of the cabin and stood at the side of the boat, taking in the stillness of the morning. A thin layer of frost coated the deck of *Perseverance*, and her breath formed misty white clouds in the cold air. To the east, a pinkish glow hinted of the coming sunrise, and a sliver of moon hovered just above the western horizon. The wind had died down during the night, and the boat drifted gently at anchor. She heard Colin moving about in the cabin and called to him.

"Hey guy, hurry it up or you'll miss a hell of a sunrise." She heard a mumbled reply and looked inside. Seated on his bunk in the lower cabin, Colin looked up and nodded a sleepy good morning.

Still below the horizon, the sun cast a brilliant orange glow on some distant clouds which seemed to float above the surface of the water. Mickey watched as the sky changed from soft pink to fiery magenta, and then the first glimmering rays of sunlight flickered briefly across the bay before disappearing behind the clouds. She didn't realize Colin had come on deck until he spoke.

"Wow! That was definitely worth getting up for, but I'm freezing my ass off."

"What a wuss," she teased him. "You're just used to that Mediterranean weather. But I'll take pity on you and crank up the engines. We'll have some heat in no time."

"If you expect to get any work out of me today, better do it before I turn into an iceberg," he replied.

Troubled Waters

Waiting for the engines to warm up, Mickey let her eyes roam the cabin, remembering how she and Pete had plotted to build the boat of their dreams. Custom built for diving, *Perseverance* had a lot of open deck space for stacking bags of sea urchins and additional room in fish-holds below deck. At the stern, the engine room hatch cover served as a platform for dive hoses and a place to get divers in and out of the water.

"You ready for me to hoist the anchor?" Colin asked.

"Yeah, let's get under way," she answered, taking a seat behind the wheel.

Stepping carefully, Colin moved up the narrow ledge which led forward past the cabin and out to the bow. Crouched by the anchor winch, he waited for her signal, then began reeling in the anchor.

As Colin made his way off the bow, Mickey steered the boat around the end of the breakwater, and when he got back inside, she pushed forward on the throttles. The engines responded with a deep throaty roar, lifting the bow upward before bringing them up on plane. Checking the compass, she turned to the northwest, a straight-line shot to Neah Bay.

Colin eased onto his seat, clutching a large bowl of cereal. "How far to Neah Bay?" he asked between bites.

"Eighteen miles. Calm as it is, we should be there in half an hour." She leaned back in her seat and relaxed, taking in the scenery. Tall bluffs formed a dusky backdrop above the gently sloping beaches with large boulders scattered along the shore. On the outgoing tide, thin strands of kelp floated like streamers in the current, and a great blue heron flapped its wings, lifted off from the beach, and settled down at the water's edge a short distance away.

At Dtokoah Point, Mickey turned into the channel leading into Neah Bay.

"Hey, isn't that a boat over there?" Colin said, pointing toward Waada Island.

"Yeah, it sure is. Wait a minute! That's the *Sheri-Lynn*. What's George doing in there?" Mickey slowed down and gave a deafening blast on the air horn as they approached, but George was nowhere in sight. His boat was drifting into the shallows near the end of the breakwater, and she was afraid that it would soon run aground.

"Rig fenders on the starboard side and get a couple of lines ready. Soon as you finish, I want you out on the bow to watch for rocks. We're going to come alongside." Mickey slid open the window at her elbow and switched on the fathometer. The props hung down four feet below the surface, and she wanted some warning if the bottom came up suddenly. Colin rushed to get the lines ready, then took a seat on the anchor winch and looked into the dark water ahead.

"Twelve feet on the meter," Mickey called out. There was tension in her voice, and she knew it wasn't only the depth that was bothering her. This didn't look right. The *Sheri-Lynn* was damn near aground, and George's engine wasn't even running. He hadn't dropped the hook, the cabin door was closed and there was no one on deck. What the hell was going on here? Mickey felt her stomach tighten into a knot. Unconsciously biting her lip, she worked the controls and brought *Perseverance* to a stop alongside the other vessel.

*   *   *   *   *

At the top of the hill leading into Neah Bay, a shiny red Corvette whipped around an old pickup truck, passing on a blind corner. Ignoring the twenty-five-mph sign, the driver punched it on the short straightaway coming into town and zipped past the entrance to the Coast Guard Station, not easing up until he reached the waterfront. With bait-n-tackle shops boarded up for winter, sections of dock stacked on shore and rows of empty pilings dotting the bay, the town looked deserted.

At the far end of town, Steve Drake turned into a gravel parking lot above the old fuel dock and gazed at the boat tied to its mooring. Sleek and racy-looking, she was the best damn boat in the fleet, and he loved owning her. Powered by three diesels, the thirty-six foot aluminum vessel was also the fastest. He and his brother, Ted, had spent a fortune to build her, but she was worth every penny. Scanning the mooring lines, Steve checked to make sure the boat was safe. Satisfied, he whipped the car around and headed back through town.

Pulling in at the Bayside Motel, Steve stopped in front of room seven and leaned on the horn. In less than thirty seconds Ted emerged, looking scruffy as usual in filthy jeans and frayed nylon jacket, long hair pulled back in a pony-tail. The last time Ted had kept him waiting, he'd gotten pissed and driven off. Steve guessed he'd learned his lesson. As Ted plopped himself down in the passenger seat, Steve gave him a disgusted look.

"Why in hell don't you buy some new clothes? You look like some bum off Pacific Ave. Don't even like having you in my car! You're gonna get the seats dirty."

"Hey, I got better things to do with my money." Stifling a yawn, Ted leaned back in the seat and stretched. "Did you get the stuff?"

"Yeah, and it's some good shit." Steve fished the small packet of cocaine from his pocket and handed it over. "Picked up a gram myself and snorted some with Margo last night. Never did get to sleep. I been flyin' high." Steve shifted into gear, leaving his foot on the brake. "What about stupid?"

"He's still crashed. He'll probably sleep til noon. Let's go, I'm starving." Ted hadn't gotten much sleep himself, but he wasn't complaining. They'd made a good haul. As soon as they'd finished offloading, Steve had collected the cash for their urchins and split for his girlfriend's place in Clallam Bay, and Ted bailed soon afterwards, leaving Bart to finish cleaning the boat by himself. Figured he could earn his pay for a change.

"You sure the money is safe at Margo's?" Ted asked, frowning.

Steve paused at the corner, waiting for a truck. He shook his head impatiently and glared at Ted. "You got a better idea? Maybe put it in the bank? Be like waving a flag to the feds. It's a hell of lot safer at Margo's than keeping it on the boat where Bart could find it. Margo won't cross me–she knows better." He revved the engine and peeled out, sending a spray of gravel toward parked cars in front of the motel.

A few blocks down the street, he pulled in at the Waterfront Café. The café was empty, except for a few customers at the counter who checked them out as they came in. Steve returned their looks with a cold stare and headed for a booth by the window. At a glance, most people wouldn't guess they were brothers. Ted was short and stocky with a heavy paunch around his middle, while Steve stood three inches taller with a lean, wiry build and short, wavy black hair. A tiny diamond stud sparkled at Steve's left ear, and a coarse stubble of beard covered his chin. Beneath bloodshot eyes there were dark circles from lack of sleep.

The waitress brought them coffee and took their breakfast orders. Steve fished a lighter from his pocket and lit up, cupping the cigarette in his hand like a joint. He took a deep drag and exhaled through his nose.

Ted grinned and raised his cup to make a toast. "Here's to twenty-five grand–tax free–and the season ain't even started yet."

Steve didn't smile. He never smiled. "That's just between me and you, so keep your big mouth shut about the money. Stupid thinks we only got a buck a pound. He finds out how much we really got, you can make up the difference out of your share."

"Hey, don't sweat it. He don't know nothin'. Bart can't even add and subtract without a calculator. Besides, he trusts us." Smiling, Ted reached across the table for the cigarettes.

The waitress returned to top off their coffee, and Steve glared at her. "Where's our damned breakfast anyway?"

"You want your steak rare instead of well done–I can bring it right out," she snapped back at him.

Not answering, he took another drag off his cigarette and blew smoke at her as she walked away.

Ignoring the exchange, Ted gazed out the window. "Hey, check it out. There's a couple of boats over by the breakwater."

Steve looked, but didn't say anything.

"Pretty shallow in there. I wonder what they're doing."

"Misery loves company," Steve muttered under his breath.

"What're ya talking about?" Ted asked, puzzled by the comment.

"I saw a boat over there when I came down the hill into town. Probably having engine trouble. I hope they both end up on the rocks," he added spitefully.

Ted grinned and nodded. "The one on this side looks like it belongs to that broad, Mickey Sutter. Kinda surprised to see her out here, since her ol' man croaked."

Steve took a swig of coffee and said, "Yeah, I hear she's gonna try and run the boat herself. Wanna bet how long she lasts?"

"Hell, with her looks, she'll just find some new stud to take over for her ol' man. Wouldn't mind a piece of that myself."

"Not me," Steve said, staring at the waitress as she set down their plates. "I like a woman who knows her place."

*   *   *   *   *

Mickey rapped on the side of *Sheri-Lynn* and called out a greeting, but got no response. It was flat calm inside the bay, and the two boats floated gently side-by-side in seven feet of water. She wasn't comfortable with the depth—only three feet of water under the outdrives—but it was safe for the moment. They hooked lines around the railing of *Sheri-Lynn* and climbed aboard.

A hatch cover lay open midship and dock lines, still attached to cleats on the starboard side, were strewn across the deck. Mickey opened the door to the cabin, stuck her head inside and called George's name. The silence was ominous. She took a deep breath to calm herself and stepped inside the spacious cabin. A burst of static erupted from the radio, and Mickey jumped at the noise. Feeling a little foolish, she started looking around. Checking the diesel stove, she found a teakettle on top, bone dry and tinkling with heat. She slid it off to one side and moved on.

"Damn it, George, where are you?" she whispered loudly. Bypassing the navigation table, Mickey moved toward the bow and peeked into the berth area. The two bottom bunks were made up with sheets and blankets, but they hadn't been slept in. Mickey tried to think of a logical explanation, something to halt the growing feeling of dread, but she couldn't. Everything that came to mind was bad. Maybe George had fallen overboard while tying up the boat. But why shut the engine down first? He wouldn't do that unless the boat was secure. It didn't make sense. Maybe he had left the boat at a dock and it came untied some-how. That thought gave her hope, but not much. Returning to the main cabin, she noticed that the loran and radar had been turned off and the key was gone from the ignition.

Shaking her head, Mickey moved toward the door and pulled it open, and immediately spotted Colin crouched by the edge of the open fishhold. He glanced up as she stepped outside, his face grim, and she stopped dead in her tracks.

"You found him." It was more of a statement than question.

Colin nodded. Mickey felt her throat tighten painfully as she walked to the edge of the hold. A loud gasp escaped her as she looked down. George lay on his back in the bottom of the hold. His eyes were open, staring lifelessly into space, his face deathly pale. One leg was bent beneath the other, and his arms lay limply at his sides.

"Ah shit, no." Mickey jumped down into the hold and put her hand gently against his skin. It was cold to the touch. She checked for a pulse, knowing she wouldn't find one. Hot tears stung her eyes, and she wiped them with her sleeve. She immediately thought of Sheri, knowing the pain it would bring. What in the world had happened? A silent sob shook her chest, and she struggled to get control.

"Come on up out of there," Colin said softly. At five-foot-four, Mickey wasn't much taller than the edge of the hold, and he extended a hand to help her up.

As they stood looking down into the hold, Colin put an arm around Mickey's shoulder and gave her a gentle hug. She felt the tears coming again and bit down hard on her lip, trying to stop them. It shouldn't matter, but she hated for anyone to see her cry. She always had. Finally getting it under control, she let out a heavy sigh.

"I'll be OK," she whispered, more to convince herself than Colin. "Guess I'd better give the Coast Guard a call, see what they want us to do."

Back aboard *Perseverance*, Mickey paused with the microphone in her hand, afraid her voice would crack when she spoke. After taking a deep breath, she worked up her nerve and keyed the mike.

"Coast Guard Neah Bay, this is *Perseverance*, over."

"Vessel calling, this is Coast Guard Station Neah Bay, over."

Mickey swallowed hard before continuing. "This is the *Perseverance*, and we just pulled alongside the *Sheri-Lynn*, out here by Waada Island. We found the owner of the boat lying in the bottom of his fishhold. He's dead," she blurted quickly, biting her lip to hold back the tears.

"*Perseverance*, this Coast Guard Neah Bay. Please give us your exact location and how many persons are on board, over."

Tears streaming down her cheeks, Mickey couldn't answer. She handed the microphone to Colin and ran outside.

Chapter *Five*

*B*y the time *Perseverance* pulled in at the Ocean Fish Pier, it was almost noon. They docked opposite the *Easy Money*, an east coast lobster boat converted for diving, and Jerry stepped out of the cabin and yelled for Mickey and Colin to come on over. As they crowded into the warm cabin, Mickey sank wearily into a seat by the door and gratefully accepted a mug of coffee from Brett, a diver who worked on the boat.

"What in the hell is going on around here?" Jerry asked. His long, shaggy hair was mashed down under a grungy baseball cap, and he sported a permanent scowl. "We heard your call to the Coast Guard on our way in. Heard you say George was dead. How did it happen?"

"I'm not sure," Mickey answered, frowning as she leaned back in her seat. "We spotted his boat early this morning, drifting close to the breakwater. Pulled alongside to check things out and found him in the bottom of his fishhold." She closed her eyes, remembering. "The Coast Guard boys seem to think he fell and bashed his head against the edge of the hold."

"Jesus Christ! George had everything going for him," Brett said. He looked at Mickey with concern. "It must have been rough for you, finding him. I mean, it hasn't been very long since…."

Mickey looked at the floor, determined not to start crying again. "Yeah. I keep thinking about Sheri," she responded softly, her voice trailing off.

"Has anyone called her yet?" Jerry asked. With his drooping handlebar mustache and bushy eyebrows, he looked like an outlaw, but Mickey knew the gruff image was all show. He was really a big softy.

"I don't know. God, I hope they don't break the news to her over the phone." Mickey shuddered at the thought and took a sip of her coffee.

They were silent for a minute, and then Jerry spoke up. "What about his boat? Where is it now?"

"After two hours of haggling over who had jurisdiction, they finally towed it over to the Coast Guard dock," Colin said. "We told them where they could find us and got the hell out of there."

"Jurisdiction? What'd ya' mean? I thought you said it was an accident." Jerry shifted the coffee pot to the edge of the stove, away from the heat.

"Yeah, that's what they're saying, but…I just can't picture it." Mickey stopped, looking troubled. "I talked to George on the radio last night, and he said he'd be here around midnight. His tender was supposed to meet him here with his truck."

"Oh yeah? Anybody seen him?" Jerry asked. "Who is he anyway?"

"I don't have a clue. Maybe George pulled in at the dock and tried to find him. But if the guy didn't show, wouldn't George just move off a ways and drop the hook? He had to be beat." Mickey paused thoughtfully. "What I can't understand is why in the world his fishhold would be open?"

"Maybe he kept his fenders in there," Brett suggested.

"I thought about that too, but they were tied to a railing on top of the cabin. And another thing; if he wasn't tied up to a dock and he wasn't anchored, why was his engine shut down? It doesn't make sense."

"Hey, you got enough things to worry about, without making yourself crazy over this." Brett was five years younger, but he spoke to her like an older brother. "We all liked George and it's really a bummer, but try not to let it get you down."

Since her husband's death, Mickey felt like half the fleet had adopted her, while the other half hoped she'd get discouraged and quit. Brett was right about having enough to worry about, but losing a friend wasn't something she could just put behind her. On top of that, she had a nagging feeling that this was no accident.

Mickey had grown pensive, and Colin decided it was a good time to change the subject. "What do you guys hear about the price?" he asked.

"Not much," Jerry answered, stretching the words out in a slow drawl. "I called and talked to all the buyers—Scott Chen, Jimmy Lee and Bruce Engals—and they all say the same thing. Whoever pays the highest price on the dock, they'll match it."

"Yeah, but it'd be nice if someone would say what that price will be. I don't trust those guys as far as I can throw them." Mickey swallowed the last of her coffee, shaking her head when Jerry offered a refill.

"Yep, yep. I know what you mean," he said.

Mickey stretched and got to her feet. "Guess we'd better go ashore and get settled in. Where are you guys staying, anyway?"

"I'm staying on the boat," Jerry answered. "But Brett's got a room at the Totem Motel—room ten."

"Us, too. We reserved one of those kitchenettes with two bedrooms." Mickey slid open the door and stepped outside. "Keep an eye on the boat for me, would ya?"

"No problem. You can buy me a beer sometime."

"You got it," Mickey said with a tired smile.

Walking east along Main Street, Mickey spotted the Totem Motel a few blocks ahead. Painted fire-engine red with black and white totems, it would be hard to miss. Trash and broken bottles littered the edge of the road, and a mangy dog sniffed at a piece of garbage in someone's yard. Coming toward them down the road, a pickup towing an aluminum boat flashed its lights, pulled alongside and stopped. The driver's window came down and Garth Lambert grinned at them cheerfully.

"How you guys doing?" Garth's friendly face was topped by a thin layer of dark hair, and he nodded as he talked. "Hey Mickey, Jim parked your truck at the Totem and left the key at the front desk. I'm headed over to top off the fuel tanks, then I'll be back to launch the boat."

"Thanks," she said. "See you when you get back."

They waited for Garth at the concrete boat ramp next to the Totem, and Mickey dreaded having to break the news. Garth and George had worked together on a few diving jobs, and they were good friends. Better he should hear it from her than someone else, she told herself. When Garth arrived, he shook hands with Colin, then gave Mickey a bear hug. Six-foot-four and wide as an ox, Garth was built like a polar bear. He wore baggy sweats and no jacket, but seemed impervious to the cold.

Garth was in a good mood, and Mickey hated to ruin it. Working up her nerve, she said, "There's something I have to tell you, Garth. On our way in this morning, we spotted George's boat over by the breakwater and went over to see what was wrong. Shit," she said, trying to think of a way to soften the blow. "There's just no easy way to say it. We went onboard and found him lying in the bottom of his fishhold. He's dead."

"You're kidding!" Garth said incredulously. "Not George. I can't believe this."

"I'm sorry to be the one telling you," she said.

"But, this is unreal. With all the rotten creeps in this business, why did it have to be George?"

"I feel the same way," she told him. They kicked clods and talked for awhile, then Mickey left to go check in at the motel.

The office was little more than a shack tacked onto the managers' apartment. Mickey could see into the living room where family photos decorated the wall and a TV was tuned to a game show. The room reeked of cigarettes, making her want to hold her breath.

The manager appeared from the next room, her hair in a mass of curlers. "What can I do for you, dear?" she asked.

"Hi. I'm Mickey Sutter and I reserved a room."

"Oh yes, I've got you down for room two. Let's see. Someone dropped off these car keys, and there's a phone message for you." She put on her glasses to read the note. "You're to call Chief McQuigan at the Makah Police Department–just as soon as you get in. You're welcome to use my phone," she added, peering curiously over the top of her glasses.

"No thank you," Mickey said politely. It was obvious the ol' biddy was dying to know what the message was about, but she'd have to score her gossip elsewhere. Mickey wrote a check for the month's rent, pocketed the room keys and left to find Colin.

He was still at the boat ramp, chatting with Garth and Jim while they launched *Kelp-Tied*. The twenty-foot diving boat was functional, but it lacked creature comforts. A small canvas cover provided little shelter from the weather, and—worst of all—there was no heater. Mickey thought about changing out of a wetsuit in forty-degree air, and it sent shivers down her spine. No thanks, she'd stick to her carpeted cabin with the heater running full blast.

After saying goodbye, Mickey and Colin drove downtown to the Makah Police Station, hidden away on a residential back street, surrounded by dilapidated homes. Most of the yards were buried in junk with tall weeds engulfing the discarded appliances and broken-down vehicles. As they entered the police station, the dispatcher looked up and asked how she could help them.

"I'm Mickey Sutter, and this is my nephew, Colin. We got a message that Chief McQuigan wanted to see us."

"Just a moment." She picked up a phone and relayed the message. "He'll be right with you."

Chief of Police Ken McQuigan stepped out of his office and invited them in. With his dark-blue uniform, 9mm pistol, short-cropped hair and a thin mustache, he looked every bit a cop. Taking a seat behind his desk, he shuffled through some papers and pulled out a manila folder.

"This a copy of the Coast Guard report regarding George Kessler's death, but I'd like to hear in your own words what happened."

Mickey started at the beginning. Colin added bits of information throughout, and together they recounted the story of finding George's body. McQuigan took notes and interrupted a few times to ask questions.

When they had finished, Mickey asked, "What happens now?"

"The Clallam County Sheriff's Department has been notified, and the Deputy Coroner is on his way. Although the accident happened on the reservation, the victim is not a tribal member, and the Sheriff's Office will have jurisdiction. We cooperate with them on cases like this, but our role is mainly to assist, however we can."

"Will they do an autopsy?" Mickey asked.

"That's up to the coroner. It's not usually requested unless there's some evidence of foul play. But in this case, it appears to have been an accident. Mr. Kessler's wife has been notified, and the Coast Guard will look after the boat until she can make some arrangements."

Mickey didn't like what she was hearing. "I've been thinking about what happened and I can't figure out why George would open his fish-hold. It was the middle of the night. Lines were rigged like he was ready to dock, but his fenders were still up on the roof of the cabin. It doesn't make any sense to me."

"I understand that he was your friend and it's hard to accept what has happened. I'm sure there's a plausible explanation. Unfortunately, we may never find out what it is." He pushed back his chair and stood up. "Thanks for coming in. I'm sure the coroner will want to speak with you. He can reach you at the Totem Motel?"

"Yes, we're staying in room two." Knowing they'd been dismissed, Mickey stood up to leave. Outside the building, Colin turned and gave her an inquiring look.

"You're really bugged by this, aren't you?"

"Maybe I'm getting worked up over nothing, but I just can't shake the feeling that something is not right." Mickey used her key to unlock the truck door.

"You need something to take your mind off it for awhile....like maybe lunch?" Colin hugged his stomach and fell against the side of the truck, feigning starvation.

"Okay. I can take a hint," she said smiling. "We'll stop at the café and grab a bite." Colin looked so relieved that Mickey had to chuckle as she climbed behind the wheel.

CHAPTER *Six*

---

*M*ickey picked at her food, not eating much, and as Colin finished off his second cheeseburger, she slid her plate across the table toward him.

"Care for some more?" she said sarcastically.

"Sure," he answered sheepishly. "Can't let it go to waste." Colin ate the rest of her sandwich and munched a few more fries. After chugging the rest of his water, he leaned back and let out a contented sigh.

"Don't get too comfortable," Mickey warned. "We've still got stuff to do to get ready for tomorrow." Colin stretched and groaned, but Mickey ignored him. She paid the bill, put two bucks on the table, and headed out. Parking in front of the motel, she reached in the pocket of her jeans, fished out a room key and handed it to Colin.

"Down this side of the building, we're the last door on the left."

Colin balanced a duffel bag on the cooler and took off with his load, while Mickey climbed into the back of the truck and started stacking items on the tailgate. It took a few trips, but soon everything was piled on the floor of the motel room. Mickey pulled back the living room drapes to let in some light, revealing a hazy view of the bay through the salt encrusted window. Her eyes followed the line of the breakwater to where they'd found George's boat. It was still hard to believe, and even harder to accept, that George was really dead. She turned from the window and surveyed the drab room. The whole place was dark and gloomy, and a damp, musty smell lingered in the air. A faded couch and rickety coffee table faced a couple of padded vinyl chairs, patched in places with duct tape, and a small T.V. with a coat-hanger antenna was mounted on the wall. In the tiny kitchen, the ancient appliances were chipped and scratched, and there were brown moisture stains in the linoleum.

Two bedrooms in the back were separated by a bathroom, but Mickey didn't have the courage to check that out just yet. Choosing a room, she tossed her duffel bag on the bed and looked around. The dim ceiling light revealed a hideous plaid bedspread in red, brown and yellow, and fake wood paneling on the walls. Mickey sighed, suddenly homesick for Port Townsend. She missed her warm, cozy house with its large picture windows and brick fireplace. But most of all, she missed Pete. Mickey had hoped that a change of scenery would help distract her from painful memories, yet here she was, feeling sorry for herself. How long would it take to stop hurting like this? Unable to answer the question, she flicked off the light and left the room.

In the kitchen, Colin had emptied the cooler, cramming everything into the tiny refrigerator—except one cold bottle of Corona which he'd left sitting on the counter. He popped the cap off the beer, took a swig and offered one to Mickey.

"No thanks," she responded. "I think I'll take a drive through town. See who else is around. You want to come with?"

"Nah, I'd rather hang out here." Colin set his beer down on the coffee table and settled down on the couch with his guitar. The familiar sight triggered unwanted memories, and Mickey felt a stabbing sense of loss. Pete had loved playing the guitar. Needing to be alone, she grabbed her jacket and went out the door.

Turning left on Main Street, Mickey headed east behind a battered old pickup and, less than a mile down the road, she turned in at the Coast Guard Station. A County Sheriff's blazer with "Deputy Coroner" stenciled on the back was parked by the dock leading out to the boats. Mickey pulled in beside it and sat there for a minute, trying to decide what she wanted to say to the man. She was still trying to picture what might have happened out there on George's boat. Was she overreacting?

Maybe it had been an accident. But if so, someone was going to have to prove it to her.

She bailed out of the truck and started down the dock. Hopefully, the coroner could answer some of her questions. Spotting the *Sheri-Lynn* up ahead, Mickey felt a surge of anger. There was no way this had been an accident! But why George? Why would anyone want to kill him?

Standing on the dock near *Sheri-Lynn* were two Coast Guard personnel in dark blue uniforms and a man in a Sheriff's uniform who Mickey took to be the coroner. One of the seamen looked up as she approached and walked towards her, frowning.

"Ma'am, this is a restricted area. I'm sorry, but you'll have to leave."

"I'm here to see the coroner." She started to brush past him, but he moved to block her path.

"It's against regulations for civilians to be on this dock."

"Oh, piss on your regulations!" Mickey said, her temper flaring. "I want to talk with the coroner, and I'm sure he wants to talk with me." The others heard the exchange and started towards them.

"What seems to be the problem here?" asked the Coast Guard officer.

"Lieutenant, I'm trying to explain that this is a restricted area, and this woman refuses to leave."

The lieutenant held up a hand, silencing him, then turned to Mickey and asked why she was there. Mickey explained who she was and repeated her request, glancing at the man in the tan uniform who was silently studying her. Stepping forward, the coroner introduced himself and reached out to shake her hand.

"I'm James Holt, Deputy Coroner. And I do have some questions for this young lady," he said.

The lieutenant nodded and started up the dock, the seaman trailing behind.

Holt suggested to Mickey that they go aboard the *Sheri-Lynn* to talk. Grabbing the side of the boat, he swung himself on deck and turned to offer her a hand, but she was already climbing over the railing.

"Thanks for coming down," he said. "The Sheriff's office has jurisdiction in this matter, and we appreciate your help." In a voice that was low-pitched and soothing, he continued. "I understand you and your nephew found the deceased aboard his vessel this morning."

Mickey was eager to tell her story, and she started at the beginning. Holt took notes, just letting her talk. Near the end, she offered a few opinions about what happened.

"So, what was George doing when he fell into the fishhold? He couldn't have been getting ready to dock his boat."

"Why not?" Holt said, interrupting her. "The dock lines indicate that he was ready to tie up somewhere."

"Because you don't shut the engine down before getting a line on the dock. You just don't do that!"

Holt didn't speak right away. Reaching inside his coat, he pulled out a corncob pipe, filled it with tobacco and struck a match, drawing deeply until it burned with a nice red glow. Taking the pipe from his mouth, he finally spoke.

"What if—and I'm just asking you to consider the possibilities–what if George came inside the bay and found his engine had overheated? Or maybe something else went wrong. Wouldn't he turn off his engine immediately?"

"There are lots of reasons why he might shut his engine down, but that doesn't explain why he'd take the key from the ignition." Her voice became louder as she fired off questions. "Besides that, why would he turn off the depth sounder and radar? I just can't think of a good reason to do that while drifting around the bay. And why in hell would he open up the fishhold?" Clearly agitated, Mickey paced the deck, waiting for some kind of response.

"You said that you spoke with George on the radio last night. Was there any mention of someone else on board?"

"No. He said his tender was driving his truck out, and he was supposed to meet him here around midnight. That was one reason he wanted to keep going."

"Do you know who the tender is?"

"No, I don't. Nobody seems to know anything about him, and no one has seen George's truck in town either."

Holt jotted something down in his notes, then looked up at her. He was almost bald, but still had thick wavy sideburns and bushy eyebrows. "That's all for now, but I may have more questions for you later. I understand you're staying in room two at the Totem. Would I find Colin there now?"

"Yes, he should be there." It dawned on Mickey that Holt hadn't given her any information, so she asked, "Is there going to be an autopsy?"

"I'll file a report with the Coroner, and he'll make a decision on that." Holt checked his watch, tucked the clipboard under his arm, and gestured toward the dock. "After you," he said.

Mickey realized she'd been dismissed—again. Leaving the Coast Guard Station, she headed into town, feeling more frustrated than ever.

At Neah Bay's only gas station, Mickey parked beside the corrugated metal building and climbed the worn concrete steps leading up to the office. Rapping lightly on the door, Mickey pushed it open and went inside. The room smelled of cigarette smoke and engine oil, and an electric heater had it warmed up to about eighty degrees. Leaning against the counter, her old friend Al was watching a football game on T.V. He looked over and smiled with recognition, the deep lines on his face giving him the look of an old sea captain.

"Well, how ya' doing, Mickey? Good to see you back. Say, I was real sorry to hear about your ol' man."

"Thanks," Mickey said, returning the smile. "I'm hanging in there. My nephew is back from the Gulf, and I'm really glad to have him on the boat with me. I guess you heard the news about George Kessler?"

He nodded, sipping his coffee. "I hear you were the one to find his body." Word traveled fast in Neah Bay and Al, having lived here most of his life, didn't miss much.

"Yeah," Mickey said and told him the story. "Hey, before I forget, tell me—how do we fuel up our boats this year? I don't see that new fuel dock you keep promising," she teased.

"Next season, you wait and see," Al said with a twinkle in his eye. For six years, he'd been telling her about a federal grant to build a new fuel dock. "Just let me know how many gallons you need. We'll drive the pump truck out on the dock."

"You sure that old dock won't cave in under your truck?" she asked grinning.

Al scoffed, waving his arm at her. "Get out of here."

Mickey said goodbye and left. Walking around the front of her truck, she stopped, eyes scanning the bay. She'd been kidding about the dock, but it really was in poor shape. As her gaze traveled the length of the dock, she was surprised to see a stack of totes out near the unloading area. Nobody used the dock anymore, so why were they there? Becoming curious, she decided to take a closer look.

Approaching the dock, Mickey noticed a boat moored a short distance away and recognized it as the *Intruder*, owned by Steve and Ted Drake. The brothers had quite a reputation as outlaw divers and they'd been cited numerous times for fisheries violations. She kept hearing they'd lose their urchin permit for one more violation, yet here they were—still in business. They raked in the money, then hired lawyers to get them off the hook.

Mickey shook her head and walked out to inspect the stack of totes near the corner of the building. The four-foot-square containers had Chen Trading Company stamped on the sides, and she wondered why Scott Chen would choose this dock to unload his urchins when Ocean Fish Pier had much better facilities. She'd heard that Chen had opened a second processing plant, so maybe he was trying to save money on unloading fees. He was certainly a chiseler when it came to the price of urchins.

Being careful where she put her feet, Mickey walked along the edge of the dock. A glimmer of purple and red caught her eye, and she kneeled for a closer look.

"These are urchin spines!" she exclaimed loudly. "And by the look of them, they haven't been here long. What the hell is going on?" Checking out the area, she found more broken spines under the hoist and on the side of the dock where a bag must have swung in against the planks. Someone had been poaching! Gripped by anger, she hurried off the dock, anxious to report it.

Mickey glanced toward the street just as a shiny red Corvette rounded the corner. The car slowed as it passed the dock, its driver staring in her direction. They locked eyes briefly, and she recognized Steve Drake before he zoomed out of sight. Staring after the car, Mickey felt a cold chill down the back of her neck.

She walked faster, hoping to catch Al before he left the station. Someone must have had access to the hoist controls, and she wanted to know who. When she reached the station it was already closed, and Al's truck was gone. Determined to tell someone about the poaching, she drove back to the motel and headed straight for the payphone. She searched her backpack for a small address book and looked up Brad Sanders' phone number.

Punching in the number, Mickey recalled the first time she had met Sanders. He'd shown up on the dock to measure urchins, digging through her entire load to find a few big ones, then lectured her about size limits—one oversize urchin could earn them a citation. Mickey thought he'd be impossible to work with, a real hard-ass, but she found out later that he gave everyone the same lecture, not citing them unless they were way out of line. All the divers grumbled and complained, but most of them started being real careful. The few who ignored the size limit had their loads confiscated and got slapped with big fines, and the honest divers were glad to finally see some enforcement.

Sanders was a good cop, dedicated to his job, and he'd given Mickey his home phone number, telling her to call anytime if there was a problem. The phone rang six times before an answering machine kicked in, and Mickey sighed. She'd been hoping for a real person. After leaving a short message about the poaching, she headed back to the room, looking forward to a hot shower and some much-needed sleep. What an incredible day! She had nearly taken off an outdrive running into a log, stumbled across evidence of poaching, and found George dead in his fishhold. It felt like she'd been here a week, instead of one day, and the season hadn't even begun.

CHAPTER *Seven*

*T*he alarm sounded at five-thirty, but Mickey was already awake. Several times during the night she'd awakened, checked the clock, then tossed and turned, trying to go back to sleep. The room was cold so she dressed quickly, pulling on several layers of clothing, and headed into the kitchen to start the coffee.

The aroma of coffee soon filled the room, and Mickey poured herself a cup, added cream and sugar, then switched on the handheld VHF. A bored voice droned out the marine forecast, and Mickey didn't pay much attention until they came to the buoy reports. The weather buoy positioned twelve miles west of Neah Bay was reporting calm winds, seas five feet every seventeen seconds. Not bad, except for the long period between waves. Mickey knew they would be slow-moving powerful swells, pushing lots of water. She switched off the radio and knocked lightly on Colin's door. A mumbled response let her know he was awake.

$*$ $*$ $*$ $*$ $*$

At six a.m. Brad Sanders rolled over in bed and silenced the alarm. He hadn't gotten nearly enough sleep, but it was Monday and he had a stack of reports to finish this morning. Sanders forced himself to get moving. His wife, Lucy, grumbled and pulled a pillow over her head. She had slept all night on the far side of the bed, as far away from him as possible. With luck, he'd be gone before she got up. The last thing he wanted to hear was more of her bitching. He was tired of catching flack for things beyond his control. Christ, she had a sour attitude, and it was always the same complaint. He spent too much time on the job and not enough time with her.

Yesterday was no different. Brad had promised to take her out for dinner and a movie, but someone called in a tip about a boat coming into Port Angeles with illegal halibut. There was no one else to cover it, and he was stuck. After hours of waiting and watching with binoculars, Sanders had finally arrested the two men, seized the load of fish and impounded their boat. Two hours later, he was finally ready to go home. The sixty-mile drive back to Forks was a slow, miserable trip, slippery patches of black ice all the way.

It was late when he got in, but Lucy had waited up. She'd started in on him as soon as he came in the door, and it turned into a bitter argument. Sanders sighed heavily. His marriage had been going downhill ever since his transfer almost a year ago. Lucy missed her family and friends back in Yakima. He knew she was unhappy, but wasn't sure what to do about it.

Whenever he suggested she get out and meet new friends, Lucy would ask him what the hell she was supposed to talk to people about. Tell them she was a card-carrying member of the Wilderness Society trapped in logger-town U.S.A.? Sanders shook his head, remembering the time they'd gone out for lunch in Forks. The rustic café was decorated with old photographs of loggers, standing proudly beside giant fallen trees. Lucy had taken one look around the room and broke out in tears. His wife hated Forks, hated the people, and especially hated the lousy weather. It rained constantly, a cold misty drizzle interrupted by heavy downpours. A glimpse of the sun was a rare event.

Sanders felt guilty that his job consumed so much of his time, but he had a huge area to cover. There was just himself and one other patrol officer out of Port Angeles, and the other guy wasn't much help. Jackson was just marking time until he retired in a couple of years, more interested in drinking coffee with the locals than staking out poachers. Sanders got mad just thinking about it.

The red light on the answering machine was blinking, and he knew the messages would be for him. Lucy rarely answered the phone, only picking up if she heard a familiar voice—but not his. She always let him talk to the machine. He pushed the button and picked up his pen, ready to take notes. A message from licensing confirmed that the person whose name he'd given them had a valid fishing permit, and then proceeded to give him details he didn't need. Sanders clicked his pen impatiently, but the next message got his attention. After introducing herself, Mickey Sutter told him in an aggravated voice about finding fresh urchin spines on a dock at Neah Bay.

Sanders remembered Mickey from the previous season when she and her husband had been diving out of Port Angeles. He had been impressed that she picked sea urchins. It was a rugged way to make a living, spending five or six hours a day underwater. He didn't know many women who could handle it—or men for that matter. And she wasn't what he'd call an industrial model either. He formed a picture in his mind to go with the voice. Medium height with a slender build, dark curly hair, pretty face. At first glance, she hadn't looked all that tough, but he'd seen her move heavy gear on the deck of the boat with surprising ease.

Mickey's report from Neah Bay complicated things, and Sanders pondered his schedule for the day. First, he had to check in at the office in Port Angeles, pick up his messages and take care of some paperwork. That meant it would be early afternoon before he could make it to Neah Bay, and he needed to have a look around the dock before any boats brought in today's load. Sanders didn't doubt that Mickey knew fresh urchin spines from old ones, but he wanted to see all the evidence himself. He had no trouble believing someone had been poaching, but proving it would be another matter.

*   *   *   *   *

The faint glow of dawn was barely visible on the horizon as Mickey followed Colin down the ramp to the boats. They didn't have much to carry since their wetsuits were already on board, and Colin had an iron grip on the small cooler loaded with sandwiches. It wasn't going to get away.

Kneeling down in front of the cabin door, Mickey fumbled in the dark, trying to fit her key into the lock. Finally managing it, she removed the metal post from the door runner and slid the door open. A scrap of paper fell to the deck, and Mickey picked it up, stepped inside the cabin and switched on the overhead light.

"What's that?" Colin asked, looking over her shoulder.

"I don't know. I just found it on the deck." She unfolded the paper and read the note out loud. "Mind your own business, hag. Unless you're in a big hurry to join your old man. Mess with me and you'll end up feeding crabs on the bottom of the bay." Mickey sucked in a sharp breath. "The nerve of that creep!" she hissed.

"Who the hell wrote this?" Colin demanded, grabbing the paper from her hand.

Scribbled in pencil, the unsigned note was written in jagged letters, all capitals. His face flushed with anger, and he looked at Mickey, waiting for her to explain.

She had told Colin about finding urchin spines on the dock the day before, but hadn't mentioned seeing Steve Drake cruise by in his Corvette. It didn't seem that important—until now. Mickey filled him in on the rest of the story. "It has to be Drake. He was staring right at me, saw me out there by the unloading area."

"This," Colin said, waving the note, "Is total bullshit. I'm going to bury that guy." There was a look in his eye that she had never seen before, and it worried her.

"He's just trying to scare me off, and—I can tell you right now—it's not gonna work. Drake's nothing but a bully, thinks he can push everyone around. But it's not gonna work with me." She took the note back, folded it up and jammed it in her pocket.

Colin wasn't ready to drop the subject. "I don't care if he means it or not. He's trying to push the wrong person. I'll take out his whole crew, sink his boat, and he'll be the one feeding crabs."

"Hey, mellow out. The last thing I need is you ending up in jail for killing the creep. Look, we'll report the whole thing to Brad Sanders and show him the note. Maybe this will be the bust that finally puts these guys away."

Colin nodded, but he didn't look happy about it.

"Come on," Mickey said, sliding into the driver's seat. "Let's go to work."

Chapter *Eight*

The sky had brightened in the east to soft pink, casting a rosy tint over the string of boats as they left the docks and motored toward the channel entrance. Overtaking the boat ahead, Perseverance skipped easily over Rough Rider's wake and roared past the slower diesel-powered vessel. Mickey gave a loud blast on the horn, slid open her window and waved as they went by. She enjoyed racing the other boats, even though it cost her a chunk of money in higher fuel bills. Rick Kautzman waved back, then shook his fist in mock outrage.

Clearing the tip of Waada Island, Mickey made a wide slow turn to the west, staying outside the kelp bed that marked a shallow reef fringing the shoreline. A pair of bald eagles sat perched in the top of an old snag, their white heads highlighted by the first rays of sunlight as the weak winter sun peeked above the horizon, adding no warmth to the crisp morning. Across the strait of Juan de Fuca to the north, the steep dark slopes of Vancouver Island showed a light dusting of snow on the higher elevations. Beyond the shelter of the island, the swells became noticeably larger, and as *Perseverance* motored over a monstrous wave, Mickey turned to Colin and grinned.

"If we can't find a place to hide from these swells, we're going to get our butts kicked today." She looked at the chart for a minute, the corner of her mouth twisting into a frown. "Let's try Chibadehl Rocks. If we can tuck in behind the reef, there'll be some shelter from the waves and we can work shallow. Plus, there won't be any current to deal with."

"Sounds good to me," Colin said eagerly. "You want me to dive first?"

"Yeah, I want to make sure everything is working right before I get in the water." Mickey squinted at him, trying to look fierce. "Just don't steal all my urchins."

Colin laughed and jumped down from his seat, heading below to suit up.

Ten minutes later, Mickey eased back on the throttles and studied the north-facing shore. The high, rocky bluffs, covered with tall evergreen trees, thick ferns and moss, were still deep in shadow, making it difficult to pick out her landmarks.

"You better go out on the bow and watch for swell rocks," Mickey said, referring to the unseen rocks which lurked just below the surface.

Wearing farmer-john wetsuit bottoms and thick rubber booties, Colin put on his flannel shirt and knit hat before leaving the warmth of the cabin. Hanging on to the railing, he made his way out to the bow, took a seat on the anchor winch and stared into the dark water ahead of the boat. After a minute, he glanced back at Mickey questioningly. "Can't see anything yet."

"Still showing thirty feet on the meter," she called out, keeping her eyes glued to the scene ahead as a large wave rolled into the small horseshoe-shaped bay. The slow-moving wall of water built in height as it passed over the shallow reef, then dropped off into deeper water on the backside. In its wake, boiling swirls erupted on the surface as the water was sucked away from the swell rocks below.

Mickey took a deep breath to calm her nerves. This was crazy. If she misjudged and got too close, the boat would be tossed upon the reef like a piece of driftwood. But this was where they found the best urchins, and lots of them—in shallow water, where most divers wouldn't go. She eased the boat closer, skirting the edge of the reef until they were tucked in behind it. When the depth dropped off to twenty-five feet, she signaled Colin to drop the anchor.

"Keep it short," she yelled and shifted into reverse to stretch out the anchor chain. The boat jerked to a stop as the anchor wedged against something solid, and Colin locked down the winch, giving Mickey a thumbs-up. The beach was close enough to throw a rock at, and she was relieved to be safely anchored.

While Colin unloaded gear from the back fishhold, Mickey started the compressor, slowly increasing the throttle before closing a valve that forced the air into the volume tank. From there, the air traveled through a set of filters and back to the stern, where it fed the 300-foot diving hoses. The engine noise inside the cabin was horrific, and Mickey was glad to step back out on deck. Grabbing one of the ring-nets, she hooked a float-bag to the center yoke and checked to make sure the drawstring at the bottom of the bag was tied. Nothing like putting urchins in the bag, only to find them falling out the bottom. She then attached a short rope from one of the davits, clipped on a wire pick-basket, and tossed the whole bundle over the side.

The gear was ready to go, and Colin began putting on his wetsuit jacket. After coating his arms with watered-down hair conditioner to make them slippery, he slid them into the sleeves and struggled to work the jacket down over his head and shoulders. His face, red with exertion, finally appeared in the opening of the hood, and he took a deep breath. "Yeah! I just love this part."

Mickey laughed and thumped him lightly on the shoulder. "Get in the water."

Sitting down on the stern of the boat, Colin pulled on his fins, then leaned back and cinched the heavy weight belt around his waist. After securing the belt for his air supply, he draped the regulator hose over a shoulder, grabbed the short whip at his waist and connected it to the long air hose. Holding his mask in place, he pulled the strap down behind his head and reached for his gloves. The three-finger mitts were clumsy, and Mickey helped to pull them on, then handed him his urchin rake. Colin stuck the regulator in his mouth, nodded at Mickey, and launched himself away from the boat, plunging feet first into the water. He floated on the surface for a moment, getting his bearings, then swam to the side of the boat and unhooked the pick basket. Turning toward the bottom, he gave a kick with his fins and disappeared from view.

A trail of bubbles marked Colin's movement below, and Mickey tossed a few coils of hose into the water, making sure he had plenty of slack. After a few moments, the stream of bubbles expanded, letting her know he was on his way up, and she waited at the side of the boat for Colin to surface with the pick basket. The wire basket, about the size of a garbage can, contained several urchins. She dumped them out on deck and used a long machete to crack open the hard spiny shells, exposing the fat strips of bright yellow-orange roe.

"They look great," Mickey said, tossing one of the cracked urchins into the water beside Colin. He looked at it briefly then let it drift towards the bottom. Grasping the rope that hung from the davit, he pulled himself up to talk.

"This looks like a good spot. Lot of big ones, but worth picking through 'em. Did you hook a gauge on the bag?"

"No, but I'll get it for you," Mickey said. She quickly dug through a gear bag for the gauge and passed it over the side. Washington had both an upper and lower size limit, and it was a pain having to measure each urchin. But after the first basket, they got an eye for it and just used the gauge for occasional checks. Colin snapped the gauge to his belt, unhooked the ring net from the davit and drifted slowly downward with the gear.

Mickey looked at her watch and made some notes in the logbook, recording location, depth and time. Stepping back outside, she scanned the surface until she spotted Colin's bubbles, and then relaxed. Her fingers were numb with cold, so she sat in front of the compressor and held her hands close to the hot exhaust pipe, taking advantage of the warm flow of air blowing off the engine. Mickey's hands were a mess, covered with nicks and cuts, and her skin was so dry, it looked like old parchment paper. The warm air felt good, and she surrendered to a yawn, her thoughts drifting to George and Sheri.

Tonight when Mickey got in, she'd call her and see how things were going. Mickey remembered waking up to face the world alone the morning after Pete had died, wishing it was just a bad dream. She must have asked herself why a thousand times. Sheri was probably going through the same kind of horrible nightmare, and Mickey wondered if the coroner had told her anything. Probably not, if her own exchange with Holt was any indication. Sheri had a right to know everything, but how much should Mickey say, when she didn't have the answers? She felt uneasy, but wasn't sure why. What the heck was it? She tried to visualize everything she'd seen on George's boat, but something was missing, and it made her feel frustrated.

But the urchin spines on the dock–now that was a different story. Mickey knew someone had been poaching, and she was sure Steve Drake was involved. The threatening note had convinced her of that. If he thought she could be scared off so easily, he was dead wrong. She didn't think it was just an empty threat, but she'd made light of it, worried that Colin might go off and do something stupid. He could be a real hothead when something pissed him off, and she didn't need that right now.

Mickey's thoughts were interrupted by Colin, yelling and splashing to get her attention. She jumped up, grabbed the dive hose and started pulling him in. Colin held onto the air hose and towed the bag of urchins to the side of the boat, then ducked below the surface and attached the line from the davit. As Mickey took up the slack, he released the float bag that had been supporting the weight and called for another bag. She tossed one over the side, and he slowly drifted out of sight.

It was noon by the time Colin emerged from the water, tired, cold and hungry, but he had filled four large nets, packed to the brim. Eager for her turn, Mickey went into the cabin to suit up. Slick with conditioner, the neoprene felt cold against her skin, and she shivered at the initial shock. The suit fit tightly, and she struggled to pull it on, working up a sweat. After securing the velcro strap at her shoulder, she slid her feet into half-inch-thick booties, grabbed her wetsuit jacket and stepped out on deck.

Colin had her gear arranged at the stern, an empty net hanging over the side, and he was already munching a thick sandwich.

"I covered the area out by the anchor pretty well," he said, talking around a mouthful of food. "Then I worked back this way, following a little canyon. There were still plenty of urchins where I left off, and it looks good behind the boat."

"Sounds great," Mickey said. She pointed at a rust-covered catamaran in the distance. "Keep an eye on those low-lifes. They saw some bags coming aboard and almost set their boat on the reef trying to get close to us. They finally gave up and anchored outside."

Colin grunted and shook his head. "That's still too close to suit me."

Between *Perseverance* and the other boat, huge swells piled up on the reef, tumbling forward in green walls of water, topped with foam. The air smelled of salt and seaweed, carried along by mist from the crashing waves. Mickey knew the swell action would get worse as the tide went out, and she hurried to get ready. With her mask in place and rake in hand, Mickey slid off the side of the boat and splashed into the water, her world changing instantly.

The silence was a welcome relief, and Mickey took a moment to look around before starting to work, barely noticing the cold water trickling into her suit. The visibility was good, twenty feet or more, and she could see all the way down the twisted strands of kelp. Thick and leafy at the surface, the strands tapered off to skinny cords, ending in root-like holdfasts on the rocks below. A large school of blue rockfish swam lazily through the kelp, and on top of the reef, bright orange starfish were scattered among patches of frilly green lettuce-kelp.

D.J. Ferguson

The reef dropped off in a deep canyon beneath the boat, and the rock walls were covered with urchins, spiny shapes merging into a dark mass in the distance. Mickey's pulse quickened at the sight. Unsnapping the bundle of gear, she started swimming, fins pumping in slow steady rhythm. As a wave swept through the canyon, she made little headway against the incoming surge of water, but soared forward when the flow switched direction. Broken urchin spines and patches of bare rock marked Colin's progress, and she saw where he'd left off. Looking for a place to anchor the ring-net, she spotted a shallow depression surrounded by boulders and dumped the air from her float bag, equalizing the pressure in her ears as she sank toward the bottom.

Mickey left the ring-net in a pile and started working down the wall of the canyon with her pick basket. Urchin rake braced against her forearm, she hooked the curved metal prongs over a spine-covered urchin and pulled. The urchin resisted, clinging to the rock with hundreds of tiny tentacles, but she pried it off and tossed it into the basket. Using the gauge, she checked a few urchins for size, then picked with a steady rhythm. Hook, pull, in-the-bag. Hook, pull, in-the-bag.

The basket filled quickly, and Mickey decided it was time to dump the urchins into the ring-net. While she was adding air to the small float-ball, a strong wave swept through the canyon and Mickey grabbed at the rocks to hold herself in place. The rush of water plucked a few urchins from the top of her basket, and she chased them down, cursing at having to pick them twice. They were hard enough to get the first time.

Holding up the rim of the ring-net, Mickey tipped the pick basket up-side-down and shook it. The urchins were wedged together in a prickly mass, and it took some violent shaking to get them out, but she was careful not to jam her hand against the sharp spines. Besides causing nasty infections, it hurt like hell to dig them out. For all her work, the small pile of urchins in the bottom of the net didn't look like much, and she set off again with the pick-basket.

Troubled Waters

Working along the upper edge of the canyon, Mickey had the strange sensation she was being watched. Sensing movement off to one side, she quickly turned her head, but saw nothing out of the ordinary. Shrugging it off, she went back to picking urchins. Hook, pull, in-the-bag. Hook, pull, in-the-bag. Her mind wandered while she worked, and Mickey found herself thinking about George again. It seemed so ironic that he should die on the deck of his boat after surviving thousands of hours working underwater, year after year. There were dozens of ways a person could be killed down here. Divers had been run over by boats, poisoned by bad air, eaten by sharks and drowned in thick kelp. But no one had died from falling into their own fishhold. What a bunch of crap!

Mickey had been over it a hundred times and she still couldn't believe that it was just a clumsy accident. George was way too careful for that. Suddenly, Mickey felt a tug on her fin and jerked around in a panic. Two huge brown eyes, perched above a whiskered nose, stared at her innocently, and then the seal gave one flip with its tail and disappeared into the kelp. Mickey began laughing hysterically, overcome with relief. Christ, that scared her.

Two hours later, Mickey was working on her third ring-net, and the muscles in her forearm ached from gripping the rake. She was chilled to the bone, so cold her teeth were chattering, but she needed two more baskets to finish up, so she pushed herself faster, trying to generate more body heat. Hook, pull, in-the-bag. Hook, pull, in-the-bag.

The narrow canyon ended abruptly in a field of gravel, no urchins in sight. Changing course, she lugged the basket up the gently sloping reef, looking for a new hotspot. The top of the reef offered no protection from the swells, but there were nice pockets of urchins hiding in the short stalks of palm kelp. Most of the urchins were perfect size, and Mickey was glad she didn't need the gauge since she had her hands full just trying to stay in place. Picking like a maniac, her basket was soon full, and she scrambled back to the ring-net to dump it.

Mickey wanted one more quick basket before calling it quits for the day. Clawing her way back to the top of the reef, she used her rake to pull herself forward through the kelp until she came to a small clearing. The rocky bottom was covered with urchins, and she instantly forgot about being cold and miserable. Popping the urchins free in rapid motion, she greedily sucked air from her regulator, then exhaled forcefully, sending a rush of air bubbles floating toward the surface. There were still urchins within easy reach, and Mickey got greedy, piling more urchins on top of the already full basket and tamping them down with her rake. Finally satisfied, she squirted air into the float-ball, hoping it would support the extra weight.

Just then a powerful wave swept across the reef, and Mickey hugged the pick-basket to her chest to keep from losing urchins. Jamming her knees against the rocks, she held on to a stalk of kelp as the water rushed past, the surge so strong it threatened to rip the mask off her face. She tucked her chin and waited for things to calm down before looking up. Seeing the cloud of tiny white bubbles near the surface, Mickey realized that the waves were breaking right on top of her and it was definitely time to get the hell out of there. Before she had time to react, the water swept back in the opposite direction, and she felt her stalk of kelp break lose from the bottom.

"Nooooo!" Mickey shouted. Swept from the bottom like a leaf in the wind, she clenched the basket with both arms, powerless to stop her movement. The blast of water sent her flying over the rocky bottom at incredible speed, and suddenly the reef disappeared from sight. Mickey held her breath as she was flipped head-over-heels in open water. Finally released from the power of the surge, she floated downward, still gripping the basket with both hands, and landed feet-first in the bottom of the canyon. She sat there for a moment, trying to catch her breath, her heart pounding wildly.

As another swell swept through the canyon, Mickey remembered her almost-full ring-net tucked away in the rocks. She hadn't lost many urchins from her pick basket, but if the net had spilled, the others would be scattered to hell and gone. Scrambling back to the ring-net, she let out a sigh of relief when she saw the bag sitting upright in its hole, still full of urchins. She dumped the urchins from her pick basket as fast as she could, then clipped the empty basket to the net and started squirting air into the large float-bag.

Before the float had enough lift to get the urchins off the bottom, a powerful wave blasted through the canyon, and the whole works tilted precariously. Mickey gritted her teeth, struggling to keep the bag from tipping and dumping half her urchins. Finally, the bag lifted free of the bottom and started for the surface, swaying gently below the float. Letting out a sigh of relief, she hooked a finger in the mesh and hitched a ride, relaxing as the bag carried her upward. Close to the surface, sunlight shimmered off the water like sparkles in a kaleidoscope, and she released some air from the float bag to slow the bag's ascent, then turned loose of the net. With a few gentle kicks she emerged into daylight, squinting at the brightness, and yelled for Colin to pull her in.

CHAPTER *Nine*

Scott Chen took his eyes off the road to check his watch. With ten miles yet to go, he was going to be late for his meeting in Neah Bay with the other processors, but that was just tough. Let them wait. He left the Lincoln's cruise control set on fifty-five and leaned back in his seat, thinking about what he planned to say. Chen had arranged the meeting with Bruce Engals and Jimmy Lee to talk about the price of urchins this season. It was time to put a stop to the divers' game of driving the price up by playing one buyer against the other. If Chen offered them a dollar, they'd get on the phone to Engals, who would raise his price by a dime, and then call him back to see if he'd go higher. Well, the greedy bastards weren't going to get away with that this time around.

This year was going to be different. Chen intended to bank a healthy profit, pay off all his debts, and establish himself as the largest urchin buyer in the Pacific Northwest. Then he'd be in a position to crush Bruce Engals and put him out of business for good. And what a sweet revenge that would be. Chen still remembered the price war two years ago when Engals had tried to bankrupt him. Soon it would be his turn to suffer.

Chen had spent the morning supervising the processing of urchins at the plant in Port Angeles, and he was pleased that things had gone smoothly. The load of urchins he'd bought from Drake had been a shakedown run for his new workers, and by the time Chen left, they were almost finished packing the roe on small wooden trays. Getting the new plant ready for the season had been a challenge, and he hadn't been home much the past few weeks. But soon, the money would start rolling in, and the headaches would all be worth it. Japan was begging for uni right now, thanks to winter storms that had shut down most of the urchin-producing ports around the world, right before the holidays when demand was highest. The first urchins to hit the market would command top dollar, and his timing would be perfect.

Too bad his wife didn't appreciate his foresight. When she learned of his plan to buy urchins out-of-season, she screamed that he was a damn fool to take such a risk. Stupid woman. All she did was complain about the way he ran the business, and then tried to tell him how it should be done. He shouldn't have told her anything. Then she wouldn't be getting herself all worked up over nothing, driving him crazy with her nagging. If anyone asked where he got the urchins, Chen would say they came from Oregon where the season was open year-round and show them some forged fish tickets. Who would ever know? The Drake brothers would never talk, and his truck driver, from down south, was paid to keep quiet. Yes, it was worth the risk. This deal alone would put him a hundred-thousand dollars ahead. She certainly wouldn't complain about that.

Chen thought about the phone call from Fisheries Officer Brad Sanders he'd received early that morning. Sanders had asked about the fish totes on the fuel dock, and Chen said he'd brought them up from Oregon getting ready for the season. When the nosy fish cop questioned him about fresh urchin spines on the dock, he told him he knew nothing about it. Let him have his suspicions—he couldn't prove anything. If Sanders had any proof, he would have shown up at the plant with a search warrant. And even if he did, Chen would simply claim the urchins came from Oregon. He told himself again that there was nothing to worry about. By morning, the urchin roe would be on its way to Tokyo, and the evidence would be gone.

Approaching the Rambler Motel where he had rented a room for the season, Chen ran a comb through his hair and checked his appearance in the rear-view mirror. His jet-black hair was neatly trimmed and the skin on his face was free of wrinkles. At five-foot-ten, he had a good build and kept himself in shape with regular games of handball. No one would guess he had just turned forty-three.

Last night in the bar at the Red Lion Inn, he'd bought drinks for a cute young blonde wearing skin-tight jeans and spike heels, and she guessed his age to be thirty-two. Chen hadn't corrected her. They were supposed to have dinner tonight, and he'd already requested a special table in the corner that offered more privacy. He would order an expensive bottle of wine, charm her with compliments and make small talk about business, just enough to impress her with his success. After dinner, he'd invite her up to his room for another round of drinks. It made him horny just thinking about it, and he pushed the thought away. That was later, and right now he needed to get his mind back on business.

They were waiting for him in front of the motel, Bruce Engals sitting behind the wheel of a silver El Dorado, and Jimmy Lee standing nearby smoking a cigarette. Pale and skinny, Jimmy wore faded jeans, tennis shoes and a lined denim jacket, and he had a permanent silly grin on his acne-scarred face. Being the youngest son in a large Korean family and the only one who spoke fluent English, he worked as a buyer for the family-owned processing plant in Tacoma.

Apologizing for being late, Chen unlocked the door to the room and invited them in. "Thank you very much for coming."

"Don't mention it," Engals replied, reaching out to shake hands.

Bruce's palm felt damp and clammy, and Chen withdrew his hand quickly, covering his revulsion with a polite smile. "Please have a seat."

Casually dressed in slacks and cashmere sweater, Engals had broad shoulders and a stocky build from lifting weights when he was younger. But he was past his prime now, and the bulky muscles had taken on a soft, pudgy look.

"I'm glad you asked for this meeting. The situation with the divers has gotten totally out of hand, and something must be done." Engals was a smooth talker, and the words flowed off his tongue like they were coated in oil. "It will be much better for us to work together, don't you agree?"

"Absolutely. We should have done this years ago." Chen kept smiling, but he was thinking how much he hated the man.

Bruce smiled in return and passed a hand through his blow-dried hair. "The divers have been calling me. They seem quite anxious for us to quote them a firm price."

"They are calling me as well," Chen said. "And my response has been that I will match the highest price on the dock. Now, we must decide just what that price is going to be, yes?"

Jimmy Lee just stood there with a stupid grin on his face, saying nothing. The feud between Chen and Engals was common knowledge, and he was secretly enjoying the exchange. No matter what they decided, it would be to his advantage to go along with it.

"So, what price are you suggesting?" Bruce asked.

"I'm sure we all agree that last season the price went much too high. And even though the market is good at the moment, we cannot expect such high prices to continue," Chen said persuasively. "So, this is my strategy, gentlemen. We start out low and insure ourselves a quick profit. If the market remains strong, then we can afford to be more generous later on."

"So, what do you think? Should we hold it at a dollar? I can do all right at that price."

Chen shook his head. "No, too high. I suggest we offer them eighty cents and leave ourselves room to negotiate."

"I don't know," Bruce said doubtfully. "Last year, we started out at a dollar, and it was up to a buck and a half within two weeks. The divers will go ballistic."

"Ah yes, but so what? What can they do? When they complain and threaten to go on strike, we raise our price to ninety cents. Let them think they win something, and they will settle down and take what we offer."

Bruce pondered for a moment. "I suppose you're right, but they won't be happy."

"Of course not," he agreed. "But what choice do they have?" No one answered immediately, and Chen knew he had them. "So, we have a deal?"

They nodded in agreement, and Chen smiled sincerely for the first time since the meeting had started.

CHAPTER *Ten*

$\mathcal{A}$t three-thirty in the afternoon, the sun was sinking behind the hills to the west as *Perseverance* returned to the harbor, and Mickey was glad to see they were one of the first boats in line. *Kelp-Tied* was already docked beneath one of the hoists at Ocean Fish Pier, and Mickey pulled back on the throttles to keep from bashing the smaller vessel against the pilings with her wake. Stopping alongside one of the ladders, she shifted into neutral and leaned her head out the window, making sure Colin had a line on the pier before shutting down the engines.

The pilings which supported the pier were too big to reach around, so Colin hugged the creosote piling with one arm to keep the boat pulled in close while he cast the end of the line around the backside. Catching the rope on his first try, he looked at Mickey and grinned.

"Did you see that? Am I good, or what?"

"If you were really good, you'd already have a line on the stern."

"Hey, I'm working on it," Colin said as he criss-crossed the rope around a cleat.

"Well, you'd better hurry before we drift out to sea." Mickey laughed as Colin scrambled to the stern and grabbed one of the pilings. Sliding the window shut, she turned off the engines and stepped out on deck.

"Since you have everything under control, hotshot, I'll go find us a buyer." Mickey grabbed the ladder and started climbing, being careful where she put her hands. The bottom rungs, exposed by the low tide, were covered with jagged barnacles and slick seaweed. There was an awful smell coming from beneath the dock—the rotten stench of discarded fish waste—and Mickey held her breath as she hurried to reach the top.

There was no activity on the dock, and she wondered why they hadn't started unloading *Kelp-Tied.* The boat was filled with a mountain of sea urchins, still draped with a tarp, and Garth's tender, Jim, was just standing there doing nothing.

"Hey, what are you guys waiting for?" Mickey yelled down. "You're holding up the show. We got a dollar bill waitin' on a nickel here."

Jim smiled briefly—very briefly—before the glum expression returned.

"The reason we haven't unloaded yet is the price. It really sucks. They're talking eighty cents, and Garth is in the office raising hell."

Mickey's jaw dropped and her mouth hung open. "You've got to be kidding! The market should be great right now. I was expecting a dollar-twenty-five. What kind of crap is this?"

Jim just shook his head, not answering. Making some quick calculations in her head, Mickey figured that they had close to three-thousand pounds on board and the difference—nearly fifty cents a pound—would cost them over thirteen-hundred bucks. Disbelief gave way to slow-burning anger. Colin was standing on the stern of the boat shaking his head, and Mickey could tell from his expression that he'd heard the news.

Garth emerged from the fish packing plant, looking grim. "They're really sticking it to us. Jimmy Lee and Bruce Engals are in there spouting off some garbage about the market being bad. They came up a nickel, to eighty-five cents, and acted like they were doing me a big favor."

Mickey didn't know what to say. She didn't want to believe it was happening. A rag-wool hat was crammed down over her wet hair, but she felt the chill creeping in around her neck. She tugged at her collar and shoved both hands into the pockets of her down vest. It was too ironic. The divers had voted to delay the season, so they could pick the quota of urchins while the market was at its peak, and now the buyers were trying to screw them.

"This is bullshit," Mickey said, summing up the situation. She looked down at the pile of urchins on Garth's boat. "What are you going to do?"

"Chen is buying at the old fuel dock. I'm going to run my boat over and talk to him. If he'll beat the price, I'll sell him my urchins." He glanced across the bay at the other dock, the corners of his mouth twisting into a grimace. "This is really the pits. We should have the boat cleaned up and be headed for the beach by now."

Garth was usually the first one in to unload, even though he was last to leave the harbor each morning. Mickey suspected that he waited for everyone else to leave, so they couldn't follow him to his hot spots. He always brought in big loads, and she figured he must pick like a madman.

A few more boats, loaded with urchins, came chugging into the bay. Mickey had passed them on her way in, racing by to be first in line to unload. Fat lot of good it did today. God, she felt exhausted. The last thing she wanted to do now was stand here in the cold, debating price with a bunch of angry divers. A hot shower and stiff drink were more what she had in mind.

Garth started down the ladder to his boat, and Mickey called after him. "Hey, give me a call on the radio, let me know what you find out over there."

"Sure. What channel are you on?"

"Come up on six-eight. I'll just sit tight until I hear from you."

"OK. It shouldn't take me long. Hopefully, I'll have some good news for you." He stepped onto the side of the boat and the small craft leaned perilously. Garth promptly shifted his weight to the center, then gave a quick wave before ducking behind the wheel.

Mickey returned to *Perseverance* and told Colin what was happening. The cabin door was closed to hold in the heat—what little remained—and they barely heard the muffled shout from above. Mickey pushed open the door and spotted Brad Sanders at the top of the ladder. It had been a year or more since she'd last seen him, but he still looked the same with his sandy brown hair shaved close to the skin and serious hazel-colored eyes in a lean hawk-like face.

Mickey raised her hand in greeting. "Come on down."

The boat leaned slightly as Sanders stepped down from the ladder, looking sharp in uniform. He wore dark-green slacks and tan shirt with green pinstriping, silver badge pinned to a shirt pocket, and a Sam Browne belt weighted down with 9mm pistol, handcuffs, flashlight, citation book, and a gauge for measuring urchins.

Mickey introduced him to Colin and fell silent, eager to hear what he had to say.

"Thanks for calling me," Sanders told her. "I've already been to the fuel dock, and you were right–there are urchin spines all over the place." His cheek bulged with a wad of snuff, and he spit over the side before continuing. "I talked to Mr. Chen this morning and asked him about his totes. He told me he brought a load of empty totes up from his Oregon plant, just getting ready for the season. When I mentioned finding urchin spines on the dock, he said they must have fallen out of the totes."

Mickey's eyes flashed with sudden anger. "Urchin spines lose their color real fast when they come out of the water, and the ones I saw couldn't have been more than a day old. And they certainly didn't fall out of a tote and get plastered to the side of the dock."

"Settle down," Brad said with an amused smile. "I agree with you. Chen sounded a bit nervous on the phone, but he came up with a plausible explanation. It's going to take some solid evidence—more than we have right now—to nail him for buying illegal urchins."

"I'd like to see you nail the divers who picked the urchins," Colin said fiercely. "Tell him about the note."

Mickey reached into her pocket, fished out the folded piece of paper and handed it to Sanders. "I didn't mention it on the phone, but when I found the urchin spines on the dock, Steve Drake happened to cruise by in his Corvette. He slowed down and stared, then took off in a hurry. This morning I find a note stuck in the door, and it had to be him. I think he's just trying to scare me."

"I'd like to keep this," Sanders said, carefully re-folding the note. A deep frown creased his forehead. "Have you told anyone else about finding the urchin spines?"

Mickey shook her head, and he nodded, looking slightly relieved.

"I'd like both of you to stay quiet about this for awhile. It will give me a chance to look into things without the whole fleet knowing there's an investigation. Chen may say something to the Drakes, but if he does, at least it will direct their attention at me instead of you. And I'm used to getting threats," Sanders added with a smile.

Colin was extremely quiet, and Mickey worried that he might be planning to do something about the note on his own, so she tried again to make light of it.

"Drake is just making noise. I don't think there's anything to worry about."

Sanders spit over the side again, then looked directly at Mickey. "The Drake brothers have a long list of fisheries violations to their names, and one more citation could cost them their diving permit and that fancy new boat. Don't under estimate someone who has that much to lose." Sanders turned to the pile of urchins on deck and lifted the edge of the tarp. "You guys watching your size?" he asked.

Colin nodded, sneaking a nervous glance at Mickey. Sanders gauged a few urchins on top of the bag and dropped the tarp back in place. "Looking good."

The radio suddenly crackled inside the cabin, and Garth's voice came booming across the airwaves. "*Perseverance* this is *Kelp-Tied*. You there, Mickey?"

"I'll catch you later," Sanders said, heading for the ladder. "Let me know if you hear anything else."

Mickey nodded and dashed into the cabin. *"Kelp-Tied* this is *Perseverance.* What's the word, Garth?"

"I'm unloading over here. Chen said he'd pay ninety cents. It's not great, but I couldn't get him to go any higher. Same song and dance about the market not being too good—over."

"Yeah, right. What we need is some real competition around this place. I can't believe the market is bad right now." Mickey paused and thought about what to do. "Since I'm first in line over here, I guess I'd better go talk to somebody. See if they'll match Chen's price—over."

"O.K. Mickey, good luck. I'd better go up on the dock and read the scale myself. See you on the beach. This is *Kelp-Tied*—clear."

Mickey climbed the ladder and went inside the large, open warehouse. A floor scale for weighing totes of seafood sat just inside the door to the left, and along the wall to the right, empty totes were stacked to the ceiling. A worker wearing full rain gear and rubber gloves shoveled ice onto a load of fish, while a forklift hoisted a stack of totes nearby. Propane exhaust fumes from the forklift temporarily masked the pervasive odor of fish, but Mickey couldn't decide which was worse as she made her way to the office at the far corner of the building. Two large windows faced the floor of the warehouse, and inside she could see Bruce Engals and Jimmy Lee seated at a small table. As Mickey entered the office, Engals jumped up to shake her hand, a phony smile plastered to his face.

"So, what's the word on price?" Mickey asked, cutting short the pleasantries.

"The market is very unstable and we must be cautious. I regret that the price may be less than you anticipated."

"Spare me your excuses and just tell me what the price is," Mickey snapped.

Bruce's smile faded. "We can only pay eighty-five cents. When the market improves, we'll raise the…"

"And you?" she asked of Jimmy Lee. "Are you in on this, too?"

"Very sorry. Can only pay eighty-five cents."

"Thanks for wasting my time. Chen's paying ninety cents. I'll be on my way."

"Wait. If he is paying ninety, I will match his price," Bruce said quickly.

Mickey glared at him a few seconds before answering. "Fine. I'll sell you my urchins."

On the floor of the warehouse, Mickey spotted a familiar face and headed his way. Doug, a full-blooded Makah, had worked at the fish dock for as long as she could remember, and Mickey liked him. He was always cheerful and friendly to the divers. Doug was short and stocky, his dark hair growing thin on top, and she guessed he must be pushing sixty. He greeted her with a warm smile.

"Good to see you. You going to unload?"

Mickey nodded. "We're selling to Engals."

"How much you got on board? You got some below deck?"

"Yeah. We have maybe three-thousand. Six bins ought to do it."

"O.K. We'll get some totes out there and get you taken care of."

Mickey scrambled back down the ladder and signaled Colin to untie the dock lines so they could ease the boat forward. Pulling against a piling, she glanced upward to judge their position under the hoist.

"That looks good," Doug yelled as he swung the davit outward and began lowering the scale toward the deck of the boat.

Colin dragged the tarp off the pile of urchins and the ones on top, sensing motion, bristled their spines in all directions. After hooking up Mickey's three bags, he gave Doug a thumbs-up and steadied the load as the groaning winch lifted the bags free of the deck. On the dock, Mickey stood back as Doug swung the davit inward, positioning the bags over the empty totes. They waited several seconds for the reading to stabilize.

"Twelve, thirty-three," Doug read aloud, jotting the number down on a small pad he kept in his shirt pocket. Mickey recorded the weight and noticed the dockhand struggling to untie the knot at the bottom of the net. The knot was quick release–but only if you knew how it worked, and Mickey showed him how to untie it, keeping tension on the ropes until she had the bag centered over the tote. With a couple quick yanks to loosen the rope, urchins began to trickle from the bag, then dumped all at once nearly filling the bin. Doug weighed the empty nets, and Mickey deducted the weight from her total.

"Arrgghh! I'm six pounds shy of twelve hundred." Leaning over the side of the dock, she yelled down to Colin, "Hey, how about donating some of your urchins?"

"I could be bribed with another batch of cookies," he said with a grin. Tossing the empty nets to one side, Colin hooked two bags from the open fishhold, making sure they cleared the deck without poking holes in hydraulic hoses or catching on a davit. He then grabbed one of the empty nets, retied the drawstring and leaned it against the side of the boat. The unloading went quickly, and Mickey followed Doug inside to sign the fish ticket and collect their money. By the time she returned, Colin was almost finished cleaning the boat.

"How did I do?" Colin asked as soon as she stepped aboard.

"Well, after deducting your donation–no, I'm kidding–you ended up with seventeen-eighty-four." She pulled a calculator from her pocket and punched in some numbers. "At sixty percent, your share comes to nine-sixty-three and change."

Colin smiled broadly. "Christ, that's more than I made in a month in the service."

"Just remember this doesn't happen every day," Mickey lectured him. "We have no idea how long the season is going to last, and the money may have to last awhile."

He nodded at the advice, but she knew it went in one ear and out the other. Colin was notoriously impractical when it came to saving money, just like his uncle. She wondered if it was some kind of genetic defect. Still, it felt damn good to be back at work, putting money in the bank, doing something she loved. Nothing could take away that feeling of success, not even the scumbag processors who were ripping them off with the price. Mickey vowed to herself to find out what she could do about that.

CHAPTER *Eleven*

---

*M*ickey unlocked the motel room door and held it open while Colin squeezed through with the bulky duffel bags containing their wetsuits. Noticing water dripping from the bags, she suggested he throw them in the shower.

"I'm going to throw myself in the shower, too," Colin said, heading for the bathroom. "If you'll find me some hangers, I'll rinse both suits while I'm in there."

"Thanks. I'll get dinner started while you're doing that. Pork chops and rice sound okay?"

"That sounds great," he answered with enthusiasm.

Before he undressed, Colin turned on the hot water in the shower full blast, but it was still running cold when he was ready to get in. Someone was going to get an earful if this dump didn't have any hot water. Waiting a few more minutes, it finally warmed up, and he stepped under the stream of water, feeling the tension in his muscles melt away in the heat. His skin felt sticky and clammy, his hair crusty with dried salt, and it felt damn good to rinse it all away. He let the water pour over his head, squirted a bit of shampoo in his hand and lathered his hair.

Rinsing away the soap, Colin looked up and noticed the spider web of cracks in the layers of paint caking the ceiling. The walls had faded to a dull yellow that seemed to absorb light, instead of reflect it, and the caulking in the corners of the shower was stained black with mildew. He tried not to think how long it must have been since the place had a thorough cleaning. Grabbing one of the wetsuits, he rinsed it inside and out, then hung it on the shower curtain rod, hoping it wouldn't come crashing down as the rod sagged under the weight.

Colin was finished but he stayed under the stream of water with his eyes closed, stalling. The hours underwater had chilled him to the core, and this was the first time he'd been warm all day. Finally, he turned off the shower, stepped out and wrapped himself in one of the oversize towels Mickey had brought from home. Looking down at the dinky motel towel he'd used as a floor mat, Colin shook his head. It would have taken five of those to dry himself.

Coming into the kitchen, Colin sniffed the air like a hound dog picking up scent and looked over Mickey's shoulder, checking the pans on the stove.

"Almost ready," she informed him. "Ten more minutes on the rice. If you'll turn off the stove when it's done, I can jump in the shower real quick. That is, if you left me any hot water."

"You better go for it before the building fills up with divers or you'll be taking a cold one for sure."

"Don't let the rice burn," Mickey said, heading out of the room.

"Hey, if I help cook dinner, does that mean I don't have to do the dishes?" he called after her.

"Turning off the stove does not constitute cooking, you little rat," she yelled back.

After they finished eating, Colin carried the dirty dishes to the sink, and Mickey collapsed into a chair in the living room. Her muscles ached with tiredness, but it was the good kind of tired, brought on by physical exertion rather than stress or a long day at the office. She knew if she closed her eyes, she'd probably fall asleep right there in the chair, but Mickey still wanted to call Sheri. Forcing herself up, she put on her warmest winter coat, a goose-down parka, and headed outside.

By the time she returned, Colin had the dishes done and was sitting on the couch strumming his guitar. Shy about the sound of his own voice, he sang the lyrics quietly. "Ripple" was an old favorite of Mickey's, and she waited for him to finish before speaking.

"Well...do you want the good news, the bad news, or the most important news?"

"Better give me the good news last, so I can be cheered up. What's the most important news?"

"They're going to do an autopsy on George. Sheri told me that Holt found wood splinters in the side of George's head that couldn't be accounted for. He referred the case to the County Coroner and they're calling in a forensic pathologist from Seattle."

Colin put down the guitar and leaned it against the couch. "Holy shit. So maybe it wasn't just an accident. But..."

"I know what you're thinking. If it wasn't....then who killed him? And why?" Mickey shook her head slowly from side to side.

"This is a mind-blower," Colin said, his face troubled. "How is Sheri taking it?"

"Hard to say. She held herself together while we were on the phone, but I think she's on the edge—keeping a lot inside. An accident's hard enough to accept, but murder? Christ, I didn't know what to say. Everything I said sounded stupid and useless."

Mickey let out a sigh and sat down in a chair. "Sheri also said that Holt asked a lot of questions about the guy George hired to tend for him. He left Anacortes on Saturday, driving George's truck, and nobody has seen or heard from him since."

"So, who is this guy?"

"Well, that's another reason Sheri is so upset. She doesn't even know his last name...just Carl somebody who hung around the docks at the marina. He helped George move his urchin nets aboard, and it turned out he was good at mending nets so George paid him twenty bucks to patch all his bags. The guy was so grateful for the money, George offered him a job tending. He didn't have any experience on diving boats, but George felt sorry for him and wanted to give him a chance."

"Do the cops think this guy whacked George?" Colin asked.

A loud knock at the door interrupted Mickey's reply and she got up to see who was there. It was Rick Kautzman off the *Rough Rider*, still wearing rubber boots and boat clothes.

"Hey, come on in," she said, glancing at her watch. "Don't tell me you just got done."

"You guessed it. We came in two hours ago and got stuck waiting to unload."

Mickey invited him to sit down. "How did you do today?"

Rick smiled sheepishly and scratched his beard. "I had a pretty good day."

"How much?" Mickey demanded.

"Thirty-four hundred."

"You little bandit! We didn't have three thousand between the two of us."

Mickey recalled when Pete had introduced Rick to urchin diving ten years earlier. After doing saturation diving in the North Sea, Rick had figured it would be a piece of cake. Wrong. The kelp had tied him in knots and shallow water swells made him feel like he was inside a washing machine. After losing an urchin rake his first day out, Rick went away hopping mad, but he was soon back to try again. Before long, he was out-picking everyone in the fleet. Pete used to moan that it had been a terrible mistake, because Rick picked too damn many urchins.

"How about a beer?" Colin offered, jumping up from the couch.

"That sounds good—if you're having one."

"You could twist my arm," he answered, heading for the kitchen. "What about you, Mickey?"

"After hearing the news from California, I'm ready for something stronger." Mickey followed him into the kitchen, filled a glass with ice and poured in a heavy shot of tequila, then topped it off with margarita mix. Colin brought the beers and sat down on the couch next to Rick. They both looked at her, waiting for her to continue.

"We," she paused for effect, "are getting screwed. I called Ben Hansen at Pacific Fresh and he says they aren't getting much product because of bad weather, but the market is strong and they're paying up to a dollar-fifty for good urchins."

Rick's dark eyes flashed with anger and he cursed softly under his breath. "I was surprised at the low price, but figured there must be some truth to what they were saying."

"This really stinks," Colin said. "We wait an extra month for the season to open, and now we get shafted."

"That was the bad news," Mickey said. "The good news is, Ben will send a truck to Neah Bay, if we can put enough boats together. He needs at least twenty-thousand pounds to make it worth the trip."

"At a buck-fifty a pound, everyone will want to sell to 'em," Colin said eagerly. "Can they have a truck here tomorrow?"

"They could, but…it's not quite that simple," Mickey replied. "Hansen will guarantee us a dollar-forty, but only for good urchins. Some of that stuff out deep is garbage. It's skinny and dark. We've got to line up divers who pick good product."

"Count me in," Rick said, taking a long swig of beer.

"Well that's six thousand pounds, just from our two boats," Colin said. "It shouldn't be too hard to get the rest."

Mickey frowned, rubbing her chin. "The problem is—as soon as word gets out that we have another buyer—the local buyers will raise their price. You can bet on it."

Rick nodded his agreement. "All the divers will be happy at the competition, but most of them won't commit. They'll wonder how long this new guy will be around and whether he'll keep buying when the weather improves down south. If the boats down there start bringing in big loads, Pacific may not want our urchins anymore. We could be left hanging."

"I asked Ben about that, and he assured me he'll keep buying as long as he's getting decent quality. If he gets more than he can handle, he'll ship the overflow to another buyer in Fort Bragg."

"Do you trust him?" Rick asked.

Mickey nodded. "Pete and I sold to him three summers in a row, and he treated us right. Yeah, I trust him."

"Then let's go for it," he said.

They chatted for awhile, sharing general news about the fleet. As soon as Rick finished his beer, he got to his feet and thanked them for the beer. "Time for me to go take a shower and think about something to eat. If I don't see you out there tomorrow, give me a shout on the radio and keep me posted."

"You bet. I'll talk to some divers in the morning and see who I can line up. Hopefully, we can have the truck here on Wednesday." Mickey got up and walked him to the door.

"That would be great," Rick said. Pausing at the door, he rested his hand on the door knob and gave Mickey a concerned look. "How are you holding up?"

"I'm doing okay," she responded with a tired smile. "Thanks for asking. The season sure got off to a rough start, but it's going to get better. It has to!" Mickey laughed and said, "I wish I could see their faces when these local processors hear about the new buyer in town."

"You won't be very popular when they find out who set it all up," he cautioned.

"And that will make us just about even." She was still smiling, but there was a hard look in her eye.

"Good luck tomorrow," Rick said, opening the door. "But not too much luck. Don't know if I could handle being out-picked by a girl," he teased.

Mickey punched him playfully on the arm and closed the door behind him.

CHAPTER *Twelve*

*D*awn came slowly Tuesday morning, and as the fading darkness gave way to gloomy gray skies, Mickey could see black clouds scudding overhead, coming low and fast out of the southwest. Clomping down the ramp toward the boats, she groaned inwardly and wished she could crawl back in bed with a good book. She hated this kind of weather. From here, the ocean looked rough and forbidding. At high tide, the huge swells piled in against the breakwater, sending green water spilling over the rocks and white spray shooting high in the air. Inside the bay, the floating docks creaked and moaned as boats shifted restlessly at their moorings. A burst of rain pelted her skin, and Mickey ducked her head, trying to hide her face from the cold drops.

In the old days—mornings like this—the divers would gather on the beach, kick clods and give each other reasons to take the day off. Sometimes they'd drive out to Cape Flattery to watch powerful waves batter the steep cliffs of eroding sandstone, and that usually ended the debate. But now, competition was the name of the game. With a quota and limited work days, common sense had gone out the window. You had to be certifiably crazy to stay in this business, Mickey grumbled to herself.

Most of the boats were still tied to the docks, confirming that she wasn't the only one who had cold feet this morning. *Rough Rider* was already gone, of course, but she knew better than to use Rick as a weather gauge. He was tougher than anybody had a right to be. Mickey heard *Easy Money*'s engine running and she quickened her pace, hoping to catch Jerry before he left.

"So that's the scoop," she said after telling him her plan to bring a buyer up from California. "We need some reliable boats to fill the truck, not these guys who will pick anything. Pacific Fresh isn't going to pay top dollar for garbage."

Mickey looked at him expectantly. "So, can I count you in?"

Jerry squirmed, looking uncomfortable, and sipped his coffee, not answering right away. "I've got a little problem. The deal is—and I don't want this to get around—I got a special arrangement with Jimmy Lee. He's been paying me a ten percent cash bonus under the table. It's a sweet deal, and I don't want to mess it up," Jerry said, twisting the end of his mustache.

"You mean to say he pays you ten percent more than the going price?"

"Yep."

"Just you, or all his other boats, too?"

"Not everybody, but I think he pays it to a few of the other boats."

Mickey shook her head and stood up. "Shit. Guess I'm wasting my time here."

"Hey, I'm sorry."

"Yeah. See you later." When she stepped aboard *Perseverance*, Colin already had the engines running, heater on full blast and a couple of fans pointed at the front windows to help clear away the fog.

"So, can we add Jerry to the list?" Colin asked.

"Nope. He's sticking with Jimmy Lee."

"What the hell, over?"

"He's got a special deal," Mickey replied, frowning.

"What do you mean?"

"That son-of-a-bitch Jimmy Lee has been paying him ten percent under the table, and Jerry doesn't want to lose that." Sliding into the driver's seat, she said, "Come on, let's go see what we can do."

Clearing the harbor entrance, they were met with fast-moving swells, wrapping around the tip of Cape Flattery from the southwest. *Perseverance* slowed as she pushed up and over an oncoming wall of water, then raced down the backside. Still behind the lee of Waada Island, Mickey knew the swells would be worse to the west, closer to the open ocean. She was disappointed that they couldn't go back to yesterday's hot spot, but those shallow reefs would be rolling with white water. As she turned the boat toward the east, Colin gave her a questioning look.

"There's no way we can work the same spot as yesterday—too rough. We'll cruise down past Sail Rock and snoop around in one of those kelp beds." Mickey turned on the wipers as a blast of rain coated the windows. "Nice day," she added sarcastically.

"Welcome to Neah Bay," Colin replied with an impish grin.

Mickey gave him a scathing look. He was way too cheerful to suit her mood this morning. But she noticed that he wasn't rushing below to suit up like he usually did, and smiled in spite of herself. Picking up the mike to the VHF, Mickey began calling some of the other divers.

*   *   *   *   *

Steve Drake chopped the air with his hand and yelled at Bart to get his attention. "Shut up a minute, would ya! There's something going on." He cranked up the volume on the VHF and eased back on the throttles. As the roar of the engines subsided, he listened intently, eyes gleaming with excitement.

A different voice boomed from the radio. "A buck-forty a pound, you say? Hey, that's good news, Mickey. I knew we should've been getting a better price. Hell, yes, I'll sell him my urchins. How many more boats do you need? Over."

Mickey's voice came back, weak but audible. "That's great, Chad. That makes five of us, so we only need a couple more boats. I'll call this evening and tell them to have a truck here tomorrow. Over."

"Sounds good. I'll pass the word to Jesse on the *Down Under*. You can add him to the list right now—I know he'll go for it. You guys have a good day. This is the *Julie Ann*—I'll be clear."

Ted Drake whooped with delight and smacked a hand against his thigh. "Hot damn. That's a fifty-cent raise."

Bart looked at him with a puzzled expression. "Lot of good it does us. Sounds to me like she was only asking certain boats."

"Listen, dumb shit, this is how it works," Steve lectured him. "I'm going to make a call and inform Mr. Chen that the situation has changed. He'll have no choice but to match the price." Steve rummaged through a pile of junk on the galley counter, looking for the cell-phone.

"Shee-it. That tight-ass Chen ain't gonna pay us no buck-forty a pound." Bart scowled resentfully, his jaw clenched tight. His mom used to talk to him in that same tone of voice and he hated it. He remembered bringing home his report cards from school, all D's and F's, and she'd say, "Just like your worthless father—dumber than a post." At seventeen, he dropped out of school and split—for good. Who needed that kinda crap. Bart glared at Steve and a note of defiance crept into his voice. "And I ain't dumb."

Steve gave him an icy look. "You haven't got a clue, Bart. Keep your mouth shut and you just might learn something." He finished dialing and waited while it rang.

"Hey, Scott, my man," he said. "I just heard some good news. The market must have taken a big jump. Word is—there's going to be a buyer here tomorrow, paying a-buck-forty."

Scott Chen almost choked on his coffee. He sputtered and cursed in Korean before getting control of himself. "But that can't be. The market is very poor right now. Who is this? No one can pay that kind of money. Someone is spreading rumors."

"Doesn't sound like a rumor to me. That broad on *Perseverance* is on the radio right now, and she's lining up boats for a California buyer. Just wanted you to know, so you can pass the word to your driver. Let him know the price went up."

"I cannot pay that kind of money. The market…"

Steve cut him off. "I've heard enough bullshit excuses about the market. The deal is, you pay us the going rate."

"This buyer just trying to get boats," Chen protested. "Soon as he gets foot in the door, he will drop price—I guarantee it."

"Name of the game, get it while you can. Price drops, it drops. But while it's up, you're gonna have to pay."

Chen's voice was high-pitched and breathless. "I already pay you big bonus this season. You being very unreasonable."

"Listen, shit-head. Either send the money or don't bother sending a truck." Steve clicked the phone off, set it down and reached for a cigarette. His face was set in a stony expression as the smoke streamed from his nostrils. He slid into the driver's seat and pushed forward on the throttles, cigarette still dangling from his mouth.

Ted smirked and gave Bart a nudge. "See? What'd I tell ya? We just got us a raise."

*　　　*　　　*　　　*　　　*

Colin was not eager to get in the water. Sitting at the stern in his wetsuit, he stared down at the milky brown water and thought about the day before when he'd been able to see bottom twenty feet below. But today, the tangled strands of bull kelp disappeared about five feet below the surface. Anchored in forty feet of water, *Perseverance* rose up on the crest of a wave, then dropped six feet into the trough as the wall of water passed gently under the boat. Out past the edge of the kelp bed, the water became choppy and the northern horizon was lost in a sea of rolling whitecaps. The wind, coming in sudden gusts, blasted down the

- 85 -

hillsides and out over the water, kicking up sheets of white spray in its path. Caught by a fresh burst of wind, the boat swung in a wild arc, pulling against the anchor line. Raindrops splattered the deck, and Mickey ducked into the cabin and put on her rain gear before stepping back outside.

"Doesn't look very inviting," Colin said as he adjusted his face mask.

"When the going gets tough, call in the Marines," Mickey said, slapping him on the shoulder. She handed him his urchin rake and cast a few coils of hose off the side.

Colin growled through his regulator and launched himself off the stern, bobbing to the surface a few feet away. Mickey tossed him a surge bag, almost hitting him in the head with it. Snagging the net, he tucked it under his left arm and started downward, following a thick wad of kelp toward the bottom.

The darkness closed in on him as he descended, and Colin wondered where the hell the bottom was. The twisted strands of kelp disappeared into the murky gloom below, making him feel as though he were swimming into a cave. A powerful swell pushed him sideways, and Colin paused, fighting to control his uneasiness. Drifting down feet first, his fins finally landed on solid ground, and he peered into the gloom. As his eyes adjusted to the dim light, he spotted the outline of some large boulders to his right, and he moved closer, looking for spiny shapes at the base of the rocks. Blast, there was nothing here.

Colin pulled himself forward between the boulders, trying to move in a straight line through the forest of kelp. He quickly became discouraged and was about to try a different direction, when he came upon a ridge. At the base of the rock wall were clusters of dark urchins, clearly visible against the pale limestone. Relieved at finding urchins, he quickly unfolded the net and began hooking urchins with his rake, his anxieties instantly forgotten.

In the rotten visibility, it was hard to judge size, and Colin used the gauge constantly, holding it close to his mask in order to see. He tossed

rejects off to one side and stuffed the keepers through the narrow opening of the surge bag. With the lyrics of an AC/DC song playing in his
head, Colin picked in sync with the imaginary music. Suddenly the rock
wall petered out, and his bag was still two-thirds empty. Looking ahead
into the dark murky water, there were no urchins in sight, and he
debated which way to go. With a heavy sigh, Colin slung the bag over
one shoulder and set off in what he hoped was the right direction.

*   *   *   *   *

Bruce Engals picked up the phone on the third ring. "Northwest
Seafood."

Chen didn't bother with normal pleasantries. "I just had a most dis-
turbing phone call. Have you heard from any divers this morning?"

Bruce chuckled, misjudging Chen's tone of voice. "Not yet. But let me
guess—the bastards have threatened to go on strike."

"No, this is much, much worse. One of my divers says a California
buyer will be here tomorrow—paying dollar-forty a pound.

Bruce tipped forward in his chair and nearly shouted into the phone.
"What? Who told you that?"

"Steve Drake called from *Intruder* a few minutes ago, demanding
more money."

"I haven't heard a thing," Bruce protested. "Maybe he's just jerking
you around."

"I do not think so." Chen rubbed his forehead, trying to ease his
pounding headache. "He overheard Mickey Sutter on the radio, asking
boats to sell to a new buyer."

"Dammit-all-to-hell! I bet she's behind this whole scheme. The trouble-making bitch has a California permit, and she goes down there
every summer. Last year, I asked her to stay here and pick sea cucum-
bers, but the snotty broad informed me she wouldn't pick slimy cukes

for any kind of money. Too bad she wasn't killed in that car wreck along with her husband."

"Yes, she is causing us much grief. But what are we going to do about it? How can we get rid of this buyer, and do it quickly?" Chen had an idea, but he was reluctant to mention it.

"Maybe we could find someone to sabotage her boat, and anyone else who decides to sell to this new guy."

"Ah, yes, that is worth considering, but it would take time to arrange," Chen said. "I was thinking we might start a price war and drive him out quickly. If the price is high, surely he must lose enthusiasm for sending a truck all this way?"

"Hmmm…that might work, but it's awful risky. We could lose a bundle of money. I'd rather wait him out. Soon as the weather improves down south, you can bet he'll abandon the boats here." Bruce doodled with his pen, making dark angry lines across a message pad.

"Okay, we wait and see what happens. But today, we stick to same price, yes?"

"Hell, yes. I'm not paying a penny more than I have to. Matter of fact, I think I'll tell my driver to check Ms. Sutter's urchins today. I'm sure he'll find some bad ones and have to lower her price to—say—eighty cents. What do you think?"

Chen laughed. "Excellent idea. I will pass word to my driver as well, in case she tries to sell to me. Tell him to lower price to seventy if she complains."

"I'll talk to Jimmy Lee. He'll go along with it." Bruce smoothed back his oily hair with one hand and narrowed his eyes. "Maybe we can get rid of her, and her pet processor. Send them scurrying back to California with their tails tucked."

Chen said good-bye, hung up the phone and stared down at the open checkbook ledger on his desk. When Steve Drake had called, he'd been adding up the monthly bills and found that his overhead had more than doubled since opening the new plant in Port Angeles.

Higher rent, long-distance phone calls, state taxes, electricity, wages–it added up to an outrageous sum of money. And now he was expected to pay the divers a dollar-forty a pound? How was he going to do that, when he couldn't even pay his bills? He slammed the ledger closed and shoved it to the corner of the desk.

One dollar and forty-cents was unthinkable. Chen needed to make a quick profit, and he needed it badly. His brother-in-law, who worked for a computer software company, had told him to buy shares in the company—as many as he could afford. But he must do it quickly, before they released their latest product–something so hot it promised to triple the value of their stock overnight. And it would have worked out perfectly, except for this meddlesome woman, Mickey Sutter. Damn her! Women should stay home where they belonged and tend to the household. They had no place in business. Chen saw his big chance slipping away, and it made him furious. Shoving back his chair, he jumped to his feet and stormed out of the office.

CHAPTER *Thirteen*

"Okay, let 'er go!" Mickey yelled from the cabin window, and Colin dropped the anchor—for the fourth time that morning. It was almost noon, and they were still looking for urchins. Seawater dripped from his wetsuit, and a cold wind robbed him of the warmth he'd generated while swimming to the end of his hose in every direction. It was the pits not being able to see where he was going. Several times he'd wound his air hose around kelp stalks until it was tied in a knot, making it necessary to surface, disconnect from his hose and wait while Mickey pulled it free and tossed it back to him.

"You sure you want to go back down?" Mickey asked him.

"Yeah, I'll give it one more try," Colin said, looking at his puny pile of urchins. A full surge bag usually weighed four hundred pounds, but these three put together probably didn't add up to five hundred. He sighed and sat down at the stern to put on his gear. Maybe he'd get lucky this time.

"It looks like a nice reef on the meter. I just hope there are urchins here," Mickey said, her voice filled with frustration.

"Oh, there probably are, but finding 'em in this rotten visibility is the problem. And I know who's to blame for that." Colin pointed at a recent clearcut on the hillsides above the beach that stretched for miles in both directions. "They cut down all the trees, and every time it rains the soil washes straight into the ocean. Stupid jerks, I can't believe they get away with it. I could be swimming by a blackout of urchins, six feet away, and never see them." Shaking his head angrily, Colin leaned back across his weight belt and latched the quick-release buckle at his waist.

"I hope it's better tomorrow." Mickey's face scrunched up in a frown. "At this rate, we'll need forty boats to fill that truck."

"Don't spend time worrying about that. You're not responsible for the weather."

"Yeah, but what if it's worse than this and we can't even work?"

"Hey, this guy Hansen knows the score. He knows we'll do the best we can," Colin said, pulling on one of his fins. "Besides, I got a good feeling about tomorrow. Whenever the price goes above a dollar, my urchin sniffer becomes ultra-sensitive," he added jokingly, trying to cheer her up.

Mickey smiled and stepped inside the cabin to start the compressor. Pete used to tell her the same thing when she fretted about the weather. Don't worry about things you can't control. But she did anyway. The noisy compressor engine drowned out the sound of wind and waves crashing on the beach, and Mickey yelled to get Colin's attention before he jumped over the side. "I'll wait half an hour and then suit up. You don't get to have all the fun, you know."

"Misery loves company," he said with a grin, then jammed the regulator into his mouth and bailed off the boat in one giant stride. Loops of hose uncoiled from the stern as he swam down through the kelp, and the stream of bubbles marked his path, meandering slowly away from the boat.

*   *   *   *   *

Deputy Coroner James Holt was eating lunch at his desk, and he'd just taken a bite from his deli sandwich when the phone rang. Glaring at the red blinking light, he swallowed the mouthful and washed it down with a swig of soda, then switched on the speaker phone.

"Holt speaking."

"Got something for you Chief," reported Lois Burns, one of their radio dispatch officers. "Deputy Patterson just called in about your APB on a Ford pickup. He located the vehicle off Highway 112, twenty-seven miles west of Port Angeles, parked on a side road leading to the Deep Creek hiking trail."

Holt shoved the remains of his sandwich off to one side and shuffled through a stack of folders on his desk, looking for the file on Kessler. "Did he say what condition the truck is in?"

"Yes, sir. It appears that the vehicle was involved in a head-on collision, probably with a deer. One headlight smashed, front grill caved in, and a punctured radiator. Patterson isn't sure where the accident occurred. He suspects the driver tried to keep going until the engine overheated, then abandoned the truck."

"Get him on the horn and ask if he checked the interior of the truck." Holt spoke calmly, but a hint of excitement crept into his voice. He could hear voices in the background while Lois relayed the message.

"Affirmative," she said, coming back on the line. "Patterson says both doors were unlocked, keys left on the floor of the cab. The interior is clean, except for a crumpled bag from Wendy's. He hasn't looked for a receipt, but figures the driver may have stopped there on his way through town."

"That can wait. Tell Patterson to stay there until the tow truck arrives and make sure no one touches anything. I want the truck checked for prints as soon as it gets here." Holt pulled at his chin while he paused to think. "And Lois, tell him to check the area for recent road kill. I want to know whether that pickup was coming or going from Neah Bay when it hit that deer."

*   *   *   *   *

Perseverance cleared the end of the pier and Mickey groaned out loud as she caught sight of the unloading area, crowded with diving vessels waiting to unload. Boats were tied beneath each hoist and along the edge of the dock, rafted together in twos and threes. The ladders were all blocked, so she eased *Perseverance* in close, casually eyeing the other boats to see how much they had on board. Doug was on the dock at the winch controls, directing two workers as they positioned empty totes beneath a hoist. Mickey stepped out on deck, cupped both hands to her face and yelled up to him.

"Yo', Doug! How many boats in front of us?"

"Hi there, Mickey. You selling to Engals again?"

She nodded yes, and he gestured toward the other hoist.

"We're unloading his boats over there, and it looks like…" Doug paused to check his list, "Six boats ahead of you. But the loads are small, so it goes pretty fast."

"Okay. I think I'll run over and take on fuel. I got time for that, don't you think?"

"Oh yeah, you got an hour or so," he replied. Pushing a button on the winch control, he began lowering the scale toward the boat below.

Mickey raised her voice to be heard over the noise. "Which boat do we follow?"

"*Grey Ghost.*"

Mickey waved in reply and stepped back inside the cabin. Dropping both engines in reverse, she backed away from the pier, spun the boat around and motored toward the old fuel dock. Leaning back in the seat, she yawned and felt the exhaustion of the day creeping up on her. She could hear Colin rummaging in the box of snacks down below and called to him.

"Hey, Colin, toss me a candy bar, would ya?" She snagged the miniature Snicker's out of the air as it came flying toward her, then peeled the wrapper and popped it in her mouth, savoring the sweetness.

Colin emerged from below with a box of crackers and parked himself on the cushioned seat. "Doesn't look like anyone else had a good day either. What do you think we ended up with?"

"I'm guessing eleven or twelve hundred—most of it yours."

"It's better than nothing, but they were damn hard to come by."

"Yeah. What a miserable day." Mickey kept hoping they'd stumble onto a hot spot, but it hadn't happened. Tossed around in muddy water with no visual bearings, she'd almost gotten seasick underwater–an event too horrible to contemplate. Mickey remembered hearing about a guy who barfed through his regulator, but she didn't want to find out how he managed to do it without drowning. Yuk! Luckily, her stomach had mellowed out once she got on the bottom.

"A long, miserable day," she added with a glance at her watch which showed quarter-to-four.

"They expecting us at the fuel dock?" Colin asked.

"I called Al this morning, but I'll try and raise him now—let him know we're on our way. It might speed things up a bit," Mickey said, reaching for the mike.

Al answered immediately, saying the truck was ready to go and he'd have the kid bring it right over. She thanked him and asked if he was going to be around for a little while.

"No one waiting at home, except an ornery ol' tomcat. Come on up. I'll be here."

Mickey signed off and focused her attention on parking the boat. While they tied up to the dock, a young Makah jumped down from the cab of the rusty old tanker and began pulling hose off a reel. Colin looked up as the hose came snaking down over the side and grabbed hold of the fuel nozzle.

The tide was low and there were no ladders on the dock, so Mickey had to stand on the roof of the cabin and clamber up over the edge. After getting to her feet and brushing off her jeans, she introduced herself to the young driver. When he didn't respond, she asked him his name.

"Name's Tim," he answered without looking at her. His long hair was pulled back in a pony tail, and there were dark stains on his jeans from wiping his hands. Stepping to the back of the truck, he turned on the pump, still avoiding her gaze.

Mickey followed him, saying, "I'd like a hundred gallons in each side, but be sure and stop it at two hundred. I'm gonna walk up and see Al, so I'll give him the check while I'm there."

Tim nodded, watching the meter as it clicked off the gallons.

Mickey knew good jobs were hard to come by on the reservation, but this guy seemed to be taking his way too seriously. Then again, maybe he was just shy. He sure wasn't a talker. She shrugged and set off toward the beach.

Al looked up as she entered the stuffy little office. "How's it going?"

"Surviving," Mickey answered tiredly. "We got our butts kicked today. We could barely see past the end of our rakes, and the urchins were hard to come by." Pulling the checkbook from the back pocket of her jeans, she asked him what she owed for two-hundred gallons.

Al switched off the T.V. and stepped over to the counter, its dusty surface cluttered with papers, a dirty ashtray, yesterday's newspaper, and a couple of soiled rags. He shifted a stack of invoices to uncover a dirty calculator, punched in some numbers and wrote out a receipt.

"So, what's on your mind?" Al asked, studying Mickey while she wrote out the check. "You look plum wore out, and I wonder what it is caused you to hike on up here when you could've paid the kid? And don't try and tell me you just wanted to chat."

"I got some things on my mind," she responded, handing him the check. "Your hired hand isn't big on conversation, is he? Almost had to pry his name out of him. How long has Tim been working for you?"

"He's a good kid. Been working for me the last few summers, pumping fuel, stacking buckets of oil, stuff like that. When he graduated from high school this fall, I hired him on full-time. His old man was a good friend of mine. Died of cancer two years ago, and the family's pretty messed up. Tim's the only one holding down a real job, and that makes it tough."

"Don't they get assistance?"

Al frowned, deepening the lines on his face, and a hard look came into his eyes.

"Some. Enough to put food on the table, but it comes with a heavy price tag. Accepting government handouts takes away a person's pride."

Mickey nodded, remembering her own statement that she'd rather become a criminal than go on welfare. And she'd only been half joking at the time.

"Well, Tim sure takes his job seriously," she said. "I think you got yourself a good worker."

"Yeah, the kid still has his pride. Wants to make something of himself." Al stared out the window for a minute. "You gonna tell me what's on your mind?"

Mickey took a deep breath and told him about finding fresh urchin spines on the dock Sunday afternoon. "Somebody was poaching urchins before the season, and they unloaded them at your dock. I think I know who it was, but I can't prove it–not yet anyway." Anger crept into her voice, and she tried to get a grip on it. Looking him in the eye, she asked bluntly, "How the hell could they use that hoist without you knowing about it?"

Al looked down, not answering for a moment. When he returned Mickey's gaze, his eyes were sad.

"Mickey, I know you work hard to make a living, and you play by the rules. Some of these guys cheat every chance they get, and then brag how much money they made. I hear 'em on the dock, acting like they're better than everyone else, when what they are is a bunch a crooks." His voice grew louder as he spoke. "No way I'd help out a poacher by letting him use my dock. I'd just as soon spit on 'em as sell 'em fuel."

"I figured that, Al. So how could they pull it off? Are the hoist controls locked up like they are at Ocean Fish?"

"The controls aren't locked, but ya can't run the hoist without getting inside the building to turn on the power. Had some trouble with vandals this summer, so I installed a deadbolt on the door."

"Who has a key?"

He paused, glancing away with a pained look. "Only myself—and Tim."

CHAPTER *Fourteen*

*I*t was almost dark when they positioned *Perseverance* under the hoist at Ocean Fish, ready to unload. Reaching inside the open door of the warehouse, Doug switched on the outside floodlights, and the north side of the pier was suddenly bathed in bright harsh lighting. Mickey looked down from the edge of the dock at the small pile of urchins on deck and shook her head. For all their effort, it was really pathetic. She just wanted the day to be over with—go home, take a hot shower, and crash.

The storm front that had battered them with wind and rain all day had moved inland, revealing blue sky to the west, and the temperature was dropping rapidly. The air already had a crisp bite to it, and Mickey expected there'd be frost on deck by morning. She tugged the rag-wool cap down over her forehead and stomped her boots on the wooden planking, trying to get some blood flowing and warm her numb toes. Her breath misted in the cold as she sipped coffee from a Styrofoam cup, courtesy of Ocean Fish. The coffee was awful—hardly any taste to it—but at least it was warm.

They were still moving totes around on the dock, and Mickey looked on while a forklift hauled away two more bins of urchins. Tom on the *Grey Ghost* had brought in a pretty good load, enough to fill five totes, and Mickey guessed that he'd been diving deep. Stepping closer, she poked around in the remaining tote and found a broken urchin. Inside were skinny strips of roe, dark orange in color and speckled with black spots. As they hauled away the last tote, Mickey shook her head in disgust, knowing Tom would get the same price she did—for a load of absolute garbage.

Several divers and crew members from the boats had gathered on the dock to socialize, and Jerry wandered over to say hello. Mickey was too tired to carry on an intelligent conversation, so she stood on the sidelines, listening to the banter.

Kurt, off the *Clam Shell,* was giving his "expert" opinion on the use of full-face-masks with communications, versus a simple mask and regulator. Once he got started on a subject, nothing could shut him up, and it drove Mickey right up the wall. She rolled her eyes and tuned him out, and thought again about George. Of all the divers in this business, why did it happen to George? Damn it, why him? She gazed into the night, immersed in somber thought.

The empty totes were finally in place, and Doug looked over at Mickey.

"You ready?" he asked.

"What are you waiting for?" she demanded, cracking a weary smile.

Doug pushed a button on the control module and the loud whine of the winch drowned out any further attempts at conversation. As the scale came down within reach, Colin grabbed the hooks and attached them to three bags on top—Mickey's grand total for the day. The partial bags formed a pitiful sight, and Mickey groaned as she read the scale. Four-hundred and twelve pounds. Oh wow. The urchins dumped easily, thudding against the bottom of the tote, and Mickey jotted down her total, minus bag weight.

Looking up, she saw Engals' driver step to the side of the tote and start pawing through her urchins. He wore a heavy parka that didn't quite conceal his bulging gut, and his long stringy hair was slicked sideways to cover a bald spot. Mickey watched as he broke open several urchins, then pushed the shells back together after looking inside. With a blank look in Mickey's direction, the driver picked up one of her urchins and tossed it back down on top of the pile.

"You got some bum urchins here. I can only pay eighty-cents for this stuff."

Unable to believe her ears, Mickey leaned over the tote and opened one of the cracked urchins. The roe was perfect! Nice and fat with a golden color.

"What the hell are you talking about? These urchins are primo!" She glared at him, but he refused to meet her gaze. "I think you better take another look, buddy."

"Eighty cents—take it or leave it." Turning away, he joined a group of divers near the other hoist.

"If you got a problem with my urchins, get over here and show me what the hell it is," Mickey hollered. He was less than twenty feet away, and she knew the jerk could hear her, but he continued to ignore her.

"Come on, asshole," she shouted at his back. "You heard me! Get over here and crack some more. Show me a bum urchin!" There was absolutely nothing wrong with her urchins, and Mickey knew it was just a bogus excuse to drop the price. She suspected that Engals had learned about the California buyer and that she was the one who set it up.

Curious about the yelling, several divers wandered over and soon a small crowd formed around the tote of urchins. Just then, the next set of bags cleared the railing on their way up.

"Hold it. Stop everything," Mickey said to Doug. She wasn't going to stand by and let this happen, not without a fight. They'd worked too hard for these urchins.

"Colin, pass the machete up," she yelled, leaning over the edge of the dock. Meeting him part way down the ladder, Mickey grabbed the long blade by its handle and clambered back up. Colin asked her what was going on, but she didn't stop to answer.

Mickey raised the blade high and brought it down on an urchin, cracking it cleanly in two. She gave the blade a quick twist, opening the shell, and looked at the golden orange roe glistening in the bright light.

"What's wrong with that one?" she hissed loudly. The blade flashed over her head as she cracked several more urchins. "And that one? And that one?"

"Looks good to me," Jerry commented wryly. Every urchin she broke was full of plump golden roe. Not a bad one in the bunch.

"Hey, I'm talking to you, asshole!" Mickey shouted at the driver. He pretended not to hear, and she swung the machete into the pile, again and again, working herself into a frenzy.

"I'll get my dime's worth," she growled, hacking at the urchins in a fit of rage. The crowd of divers backed up about four paces, but Mickey barely noticed, anger engulfing her like a fog.

"Hey, Colin, I think you better come up here and get this machete—before she kills somebody," Jerry yelled.

Mickey heard the comment and suddenly became aware of her audience, ten or more men standing in a wide circle around the tote. Letting the blade drop to her side, she glanced at their faces as they looked on in stunned silence. Colin appeared at Mickey's elbow, and she handed him the machete without saying a word. Heart pounding in her chest, she suddenly felt shaky and braced herself against the tote.

Two of Colin's bags were still suspended from the hoist, resting against the edge of the dock, and everyone waited silently to see what she'd do next. Mickey took a deep breath, turned to Colin, and spoke in what she hoped was a normal voice.

"We'll hang the rest of our urchins in the water–save 'em for tomorrow."

Doug still held the hoist controls, and she asked him to lower the two bags back down to the boat.

"What about those?" Doug asked, pointing toward the bin of massacred urchins.

"You heard the man. He offered me eighty-cents, and I guess I'll take it." She noticed a few raised eyebrows, but Doug smiled and nodded his head.

"Okay with me."

Mickey managed to keep a straight face as she turned and entered the warehouse, then allowed herself a private smile. This was going to cost Engals a lot more than it was costing her. Inside the office, she handed over her license card to Carla who filled out the fish ticket. Still shaky from the rush of emotions, Mickey's hand trembled as she signed her name at the bottom of the form. A few minutes later, she collected her check for three-hundred-and-twelve dollars, written against Engals' account, and hurried back to the boat.

It was pitch black outside when Mickey steered *Perseverance* around the end of the pier and slipped in at the dock behind *Kelp-Tied*. Working under the glare of two halogen deck lights, they used the crane to lower the bags of urchins into the water, tied them off to cleats at the side of the boat, then tossed their gear into the rear hold and gave the deck a quick rinse down.

"Good enough," Mickey said, stepping inside to turn off the pump.

Colin rubbed his hands together as he entered the warm cabin.

"Damn cold out there," he said, then smiled at a sudden thought. "But it was pretty hot while you were swinging that machete."

Mickey nodded and started chuckling. "You should have seen the looks on their faces."

"I did. But you should've seen what you looked like. A maniac woman with a machete." They started laughing, and Mickey felt a welcome release from the tension.

"I can't believe you sold him those urchins after hacking them up," Colin said, doubling up with laughter.

"The creep didn't want to deal with me."

"Hell, he was afraid to after that." Colin wiped the tears from his eyes, and Mickey leaned against the seat, holding her sides.

"Stop it, you're killing me," she said, trying to keep the grin off her face.

They got it under control for a few seconds, then made the mistake of looking at each other and broke out in a new wave of laughter, unable to stop themselves. A couple of minutes passed before Mickey trusted herself to speak.

"Come on, let's get out of here."

CHAPTER *Fifteen*

*B*ack at the room, Mickey poured herself a stiff margarita, opened a beer for Colin, and carried them into the living room. Leaning back on the couch, she closed her eyes and felt herself melt against the cushions.

"What's for dinner?" Colin asked, trying to sound casual.

Mickey groaned. "Whatever you want to fix," she said with a hint of sarcasm. "On second thought, I take that back. I don't really want a peanut butter sandwich for dinner. I've got a better idea. Let's walk down to the café after we get cleaned up. How's that sound?"

"No problem. If you're too lazy to cook, I understand," he teased.

"Just for that, you little rat, I'm taking the first shower and you get to buy dinner."

Mickey emerged from the bathroom fifteen minutes later, feeling refreshed. Her towel-dried hair was parted down the middle, and she wore a dark green turtleneck, wool sweater and tan denims. She found Colin doing pushups in the middle of the living room floor and shook her head in amazement.

"I don't believe this. Didn't you get enough of a workout today?"

Colin finished the set and bounced to his feet, grinning.

"Hey, listen at this. I figured out where I can put my weight set. It will fit right here between the couch and the chair. What do you think?"

"I think you've soaked your head in saltwater too long," Mickey said. "I also think I'm starving, and I think I'll go eat while you stay here and do pushups."

"Give me five minutes," he said and dashed for the shower.

The Waterfront Cafe was busy and most of the tables were taken when Mickey and Colin arrived. Scanning the room, they spotted Rick and Chad at a booth by the window and wandered over to say hi.

"Grab a seat," Chad said, scooting over to make room. "We haven't ordered."

Mickey and Colin sat down and looked over the menu.

"Guess we missed all the excitement today," Rick said, giving Mickey a mischievous look. "Rumor on the dock has it that you went after Engals' driver with a machete."

"No, that isn't what happened," Mickey protested. "But, I kinda wish I had," she added with a grin.

"So, tell us the real story."

Mickey started to give her version of the story, toning it down just slightly, but Colin interrupted and launched into a spirited description, waving his arms to imitate the action.

"And then she really went berserk. The divers—all these big guys—started backing up, wondering what she'd do next. You should've seen her. It was awesome."

Mickey was embarrassed and wished Colin would shut up. She was usually pretty cool about things, but when Engals' driver said eighty cents, she'd totally lost it. Colin told the story like she was some kind of hero, and it made Mickey want to hide behind her menu. Asking him to order the prawns for her, she escaped outside, saying she had to make a call.

*   *   *   *   *

Brad Sanders was just sitting down to dinner when the phone rang. He caught the sudden flash of resentment on Lucy's face and thought about letting the answering machine pick it up, then remembered he'd switched it off when he checked his messages. Brad pushed back from the table, crossed the room in three strides and picked it up on the fourth ring.

"Sanders here."

"Hi, Brad, this is Mickey. Sorry to bother you at home, but I've got some important news for you. Hope this isn't a bad time."

"No, it's all right," he answered, glancing at Lucy. She was staring down at her plate, chewing her food in angry silence. Brad sighed inwardly and returned his attention to Mickey who was excitedly telling him about her conversation with Al.

"They couldn't unload at the fuel dock without getting inside the building to turn on the power, and Tim is the only person besides Al who has a key. I'm convinced Al didn't know anything about it. He seemed pretty upset."

"Sounds like I better have a chat with Tim. If he'll identify the boat and divers, I may have enough to take to the prosecutor."

"It's a touchy situation. Al thinks the world of Tim and doesn't want to get him in trouble. He reluctantly admitted that Tim is hurting for money, trying to save up enough to get his own place. I tried to convince him that it's the poachers you're after, not Tim. It` might help if you reassure him of that."

"Is Tim a Makah?"

"Yes."

"Then he's probably in the clear. Technically, he wasn't involved in the actual poaching, and we usually don't have jurisdiction on the reservation anyway—unless a federal law is broken, and then the FBI gets involved. The only violations I'll be pursuing involve the boat crew and the processor who bought the urchins." Brad felt a rush of adrenaline. The case was coming together, and he loved the excitement. "Did Al say whether Tim would be willing to talk to me?"

"No. Tim came in right before I left, and I had the impression Al was still trying to decide how to handle it. Maybe they talked, I don't know."

D.J. Ferguson

"I'll speak with Al first, let him know there's nothing to worry about," Sanders said. "Hopefully, he'll help persuade Tim to make a statement."

"I think that's a good idea. Tim is pretty close-mouthed," Mickey said. "I sure hope you get him to talk."

"Don't worry. I'll find a way." Brad paused and thought about his schedule the next day. "I'll be out there as early as I can tomorrow. Keep this to yourself, okay?"

"Colin is the only one I've told, and we'll keep it quiet. We want you to nail these bastards."

"I don't deserve the credit for this one," he said. "Thanks for all your help."

"If you can put the Drake brothers in jail, that's all the thanks I need."

Sanders laughed. "Take care Mickey, and I'll try to catch up with you tomorrow."

"Let me know what happens," she said eagerly.

"I will. Good night."

Lucy had finished eating while Brad was still on the phone, and now she took her empty plate into the kitchen. When she returned, Brad started to apologize for missing dinner, but Lucy gave him an angry look and went into the bedroom, shutting the door with a firm thud.

Good night indeed, he thought, shaking his head.

*   *   *   *   *

The others had finished their soup by the time Mickey got back to the table, and she started on hers without a word.

"Must have been something important to keep you away from food," Rick said, noticing that she was inhaling the small bowl of clam chowder.

"Yes, it was." Mickey used a napkin to wipe her mouth and set the empty bowl to the side. "It's good news. But I can't tell you about it— not yet anyway." She smiled, her eyes sparkling with excitement.

"Why not? What the devil is going on?" Rick asked.

"Sorry, I promised not to talk about it."

Just then the waitress arrived with their dinners, and Mickey, thankful for the interruption, dipped one of her fried prawns in cocktail sauce and bit into it hungrily. Armed with knife and fork, Colin went to work on a giant T-bone, accompanied by a baked potato, corn and dinner roll. Preoccupied with eating, no one spoke for awhile.

"That's it for me," Mickey said, shoving away the remains of her baked potato. Colin, Rick and Chad ordered apple pie topped with vanilla ice cream for dessert, but Mickey passed, settling for a cup of coffee instead.

"So, are we on for tomorrow?" Rick asked.

"You bet. Pacific Fresh will have a truck here by three o'clock," Mickey said, stirring her coffee.

"How many boats have you got lined up?" Chad asked.

"Eight. That should be enough, but if it's lousy weather like it was today…I don't know. Be nice to have a couple more," she added.

"Forecast calls for east wind, but the swell is supposed to come down," Chad said. "And it quit raining, so maybe the visibility will improve."

"Yeah, it'll probably be great during the closure," she stated sarcastically. "Speaking of that, what are you guys doing during our days off? Going to hang around or head back to Port Townsend?"

"I need to fix a few things on the boat, and then I plan to head home," Rick answered. "How about you?"

"Haven't decided. I'd feel better about leaving if I knew someone would be here to look after the boats. But the reason I'm asking is, I'd like to have you guys over for a big lasagna feed, maybe invite Garth and Jerry, too. How does tomorrow night sound?"

Rick nodded thoughtfully. "I need to take on fuel when I come in, so it might be seven-thirty, eight-o'clock before we get there. Is that too late?"

"No. That'll give me time to get things ready. Let's do it." Mickey drained her coffee cup and reached for the bill.

"Oh no, this one's on me," Rick said, snatching the bill from her hand.

Mickey started to protest, but saw it wasn't going to do any good, so she gave up and thanked him for dinner.

Once they were outside, Mickey gave Colin a wry look. "Well, you sure managed to skate on that one, you little rat," she said.

"Luck of the draw," he said with a grin.

CHAPTER *Sixteen*

*N*eah Bay sparkled with tiny diamonds as the first rays of sunlight played across the water. The bay was calm, mirroring a clear blue sky, but the magic of the morning was lost on Mickey. She was running late. Of all the blasted days to oversleep. She knew better than to close her eyes again after the alarm went off, but it had felt so good to lay there, resting her sore muscles for just a wee bit longer. Forty-five minutes later, she woke up, looked at the clock and bounced out of bed in a panic, cursing herself.

Mickey parked the truck near the head of the pier and with a quick scan of the harbor, saw that most of the boats had already left. She and Colin grabbed their wetsuits out of the back of the truck and hurried out on the pier. Mickey spotted Garth up ahead on the ramp leading down to the boats, and she shouted to get his attention. He had a can of outboard fuel in one hand and gripped the railing with the other, trying to keep his footing on the frosty planks. At the bottom of the ramp, he stopped and waited for them to catch up.

"Hey, it's the machete woman," Garth said with a grin. "Looks like a nice day. So, why aren't you gone by now?"

"We hung around so we could follow you to your hot spot," Mickey responded, keeping a straight face.

"That's cool," he said. "I found some good picking yesterday, right outside the harbor, and there's still a lot there. Come on out. I'll show you where it's at."

"I was only kidding," she said, a little flustered.

"I wasn't. I'd rather you guys helped me pick it, than these jerks who try to seagull me every day. I took my time this morning, waiting for them to leave. Let 'em follow somebody else for a change."

Seeing the eager look on Colin's face, Mickey decided to accept the offer.

"Thanks, we'll return the favor sometime. After yesterday, we can sure use a good day."

"You've already done us a favor, getting a new buyer up here. We on for today?"

"You bet. Ben said the truck would be here by three, and he's already made arrangements with Ocean Fish. Just come in and tell 'em you're selling to Pacific." Mickey hoisted her wetsuit bag, ready to get going.

When they reached *Kelp-Tied*, Garth handed the gas can to Jim, lifting it casually with one hand as though it were empty, then turned back toward Mickey.

"When you come out of the harbor, go east half-a-mile and you'll see me tucked in near shore. There's a couple of shallow reefs you have to cross, but you shouldn't have any trouble. Pull alongside, and I'll point out where I already worked."

"Okay, we'll be right behind you, soon as we load these bags." Mickey started away, then remembered dinner. "Hey, you and Jim are invited over for lasagna after work tonight. I figure we're overdue for some fun around here."

"You got that right," Garth said as he climbed aboard. "Sounds like a plan."

*　　*　　*　　*　　*

James Holt laid his pipe in the ashtray and forced his attention back to the report he was writing. God, he hated paperwork. Times had changed since he'd joined the force twenty years ago, and it seemed like he spent most of his time filling out forms. At age fifty-five, he could take an early retirement, but the thought of spending his days at home with Mary and her soap operas didn't appeal to him at all.

Holt looked up as his boss, Detective-Sgt. Vern Goodwin, stepped into the room. Goodwin was ten years younger than Holt, and he'd been with the department less than two years, an import from Phoenix P.D. It had rankled Holt when the brass hired an outsider to become head of detectives, but he had to admit—they could've done worse.

"Morning, James," Goodwin said. "How's your case load right now?"

"Too damn much paperwork, but other than that, it's not bad. Why? What's up?"

"I sat in on Kessler's autopsy yesterday. The pathologist isn't finished with his final report yet, but I'm upgrading this case to a homicide."

Holt leaned forward in his chair. "What did you find?"

"Well, you were right about those fibers in the head wound—they came from a wooden object and nothing on the boat matches up. The initial blow to the side of the head may have caused the victim to lose consciousness, but the impact of hitting the deck fractured the rear of the skull and caused massive hemorrhaging. Probably killed him within minutes. But it had to be quite a fall. Slipping and falling on deck—even into a fishhold—wouldn't have caused that much damage." Goodwin paused, smoothing his mustache as he gazed at Holt. "Have you come up with anything on that deck hand?"

Holt told him about finding Kessler's truck. "We got some good prints off it, and we're running them now. There was also a receipt from Wendy's for burgers and fries, stamped with the date and time—seven-thirty Saturday evening. Which means Carl could have been in Neah Bay by nine-o'clock. Do we have an estimated time of death?"

"The pathologist will try to narrow it down, but the rough estimate is between one and three a.m. on Sunday."

Holt stared at the ceiling for a moment. "It appears that Carl hit a deer, then abandoned the truck when it overheated. I had Patterson check the area for recent road kill, and he found a deer alongside the road, about half a mile to the west. Which leads me to believe, Carl was on his way back from Neah Bay." Holt spoke calmly, but his pulse quickened as he thought of the implications. "If Carl drove straight there after stopping at Wendy's, he would've had a few hours to kill in Neah Bay before Kessler got there with the boat. Maybe someone will remember seeing the truck."

"Get a deputy out there to check on that," Goodwin said, his eyes fixed on Holt, then added, "Make this case your top priority and keep me informed. I want this guy Carl found immediately."

*   *   *   *   *

In the office at the fuel depot, Brad Sanders fell silent and waited for Al to respond. Brad had done his best to convince him, but he wasn't sure it had worked. Deep in thought, Al stared out the window overlooking the bay and watched the birds feeding along the shoreline. Farther out, a harbor seal popped its head up, then disappeared, leaving a circular ripple on the surface. The long silence was finally broken by the rumbling of a fuel truck outside.

At the sound of footsteps, Al turned from the window and faced the door. Tim stepped inside, clutching a wad of delivery receipts, and glanced warily at Sanders, taking in the uniform and badge. He gave Al a questioning look, but said nothing.

Al sighed before speaking. "Tim, this is Officer Sanders from Fish and Wildlife. I'd like you to repeat to him what you told me last night."

An alarmed look crossed Tim's face, and he shook his head, short pony-tail swinging with the motion.

Al spoke to him quietly, but there was a note of insistence beneath the persuasive tone. "It's all right. You're not in any trouble. Just tell him what happened Saturday night."

Reluctantly, Tim told Sanders about being approached by one of the divers off *Intruder* a week before the season started. "He offered me two hundred bucks to run the hoist, and told me to be there at midnight, ready to go." Tim stared at the floor and added, "I needed the money."

"The truck that picked up the urchins, was it from Chen Trading Company?" Brad asked, keeping his voice neutral.

"No, it was a rental, but the totes were Chen's. His truck dropped them off Saturday morning, and we used a bunch that night. Biggest pile of urchins I've ever seen on a boat. They didn't get in until twelve-thirty, so we got a late start, and it took hours to get 'em unloaded."

"Can you tell me many pounds they had?"

"I counted bins while I was loading the truck, and there was thirty of 'em. Must've been about twenty-thousand pounds. Made me feel really stupid, 'cause they normally pay two cents a pound to unload. If I'd had any idea how much they were bringing in…." He glanced quickly at Al, then looked away.

"Who all was there that night?"

Tim spoke softly, his eyes shifting around the room restlessly. "There were three of 'em on the boat, the two Drake brothers and the one they call Bart. And then there was the guy driving the truck. Some oriental dude. He didn't talk much, just read the scale and kept track of the weight."

"The driver, is he the same one picking up Chen's urchins this week?"

"No, he only showed up that one night, and I don't remember much about him, except that he was small—smaller than me—with dark hair. Chen's regular driver is a big, burly white guy."

"Who paid you, the truck driver?"

Tim snorted and shook his head. "No, my deal was with Steve Drake. Soon as they came in with the boat, I told him I wouldn't start unloading 'til I got my money—up front. He told me I'd get paid afterwards, but I didn't trust him. We argued, and I threatened to go home. For a second, I thought he was going to deck me, but he stormed off and came back with the cash."

Sanders nodded and waited for him to continue.

"After we got all the bags dumped, I used the forklift to load the totes and the minute I finished, that driver was out of there. I guess the Drakes had already split, cause Bart was down there by himself puttin' away gear. I locked up and went home."

Brad Sanders looked up from his notes. "And what time was that?"

"Must have been about three-thirty." Tim shifted his weight from one foot to the other and checked his watch. "Are we almost finished? I'm supposed to make a few more deliveries before lunch."

"Just a couple more questions, and I'll let you go." Brad ran his pen down the edge of the pad, scanning his notes. "The rental truck, do you remember the name of the company?"

Tim frowned, trying to picture it. "It was yellow, an' I think the name started with an 'R.'" He paused, then shrugged. "I'm really not sure. But it had Oregon plates on it—that much I remember."

Sanders wrote that down before continuing. "You said Steve Drake approached you a week before the season. Was the *Intruder* already here?"

"Nah, it showed up a few days later."

"That's right," Al said, interrupting for the first time. "*Intruder* got here on Wednesday. I remember because they bought fuel the day they arrived and made a point of saying they were here to do some surveying. I didn't think anything about it when they came and went from the harbor the next couple of days."

Finishing up, Sanders read his notes out loud, then asked Tim to sign at the bottom. He thanked him for his help, and Tim was out the door in a flash.

Al leaned forward and put his elbows on the counter.

"So, what happens now?" he asked.

"A little legwork on my part. I'll ask around, try to find someone to back up Tim's story. Maybe a fisherman saw the *Intruder* out diving last week."

"For Christ's sake, you got an eyewitness. What more do you need?"

"I've probably got enough for warrants on *Intruder* and all the crew, but I'll need more to bring charges against Chen. I want this case to be rock solid. One more felony conviction will cost the Drake brothers their permit and that fancy new boat they just dumped a quarter-million dollars into. And you can bet they'll hire the best lawyer in town to fight it."

Al frowned as he thought of something else. "If the Drakes find out that it was Tim who fingered them, I don't like to think what they might do."

Sanders nodded and a hard look came into his eyes. "I'll keep it quiet as long as I can, but when it goes to trial, they'll find out. By then, I intend to have the deck stacked against them, so it'll be just one more card. We get this case before the right judge, they'll have a couple of years in prison to cool off."

"I hope you're right," Al said, rubbing the whiskers on his chin. "What kind of time frame you figure on this thing?"

"Depends what else I can dig up today, but with a little luck, I'll be back tonight with warrants." Sanders put on his hat and started for the door.

"Sounds good," Al said, straightening up. "I'll be looking for you."

CHAPTER *Seventeen*

*B*eams of sunlight filtered down through the water, reminding Mickey of morning sun in a misty forest, with miniature trees of palm kelp swaying back and forth in the slow-moving swells. A series of shallow reefs ran parallel to shore, and Mickey hunkered in one of the canyons, sheltered from the brunt of the waves. Every nook and cranny was filled with dense, heavy urchins, and she braced herself against the rocks while stuffing urchins through the narrow opening of the surge bag. Hook, pull, in-the-bag. Hook, pull, in-the-bag. Keeping pace with an upbeat Kenny G tune playing inside her head, she worked her way along the ridge.

Mickey wrestled with the nearly full bag, trying to move it forward, but a piece of mesh was hung up on the rocks. Aggravated by the slow down, she whipped around to free it and slammed her elbow into an urchin. A burning sensation shot up her arm as the sharp spine imbedded itself in the skin above her elbow. Ah shit, that hurt. And it would hurt more later when she had to dig it out with a needle and tweezers. Hopefully, it would come out in one piece. Urchin spines had a nasty habit of breaking off, and the tiniest sliver would cause an infection.

Moving carefully this time, she reached back to unhook the net and boosted it onto her knees, grunting with the effort. Keeping the bag up off the bottom, she humped it forward until she reached the next cluster of urchins, then picked up the pace again. Hook, pull, in-the-bag. Hook, pull, in-the-bag.

Mickey chuckled to herself, remembering what a foul mood she'd started with that morning. Showing up late had turned out to be a stroke of good luck, and they were having a great day. Colin had stuffed four quick bags before Mickey ordered him out of the water, knowing he'd stay down all day, if she let him. She was working on her third bag and planned to fill another. With the urchins from yesterday, they'd have quite a load, and selling them all at a dollar-forty a pound was going to make it a super pay day. The kind of day that made it all worthwhile.

A short distance away, Mickey saw a stream of bubbles rising toward the surface and knew it had to be Garth working his way down the same canyon. She waved as he came into view, swinging her rake in a wide arc. He returned her wave, then started heading back the way he'd come. Leaving her bag, she quickly swam over, tapped him on the shoulder to get his attention, then pointed back toward her bag, cupping her arms in a wide circle, and gestured toward the surface. She wanted him to understand that her bag was full and she was leaving. Garth nodded, giving her a thumbs up, and then set to work filling his bag. Mickey watched for a minute, amazed at how fast he moved. The guy might be a slow-moving bear on land, but underwater, he was like a piranha in a feeding frenzy.

Mickey swam back to her bag and topped it off, cramming in urchins until the mesh was stretched to the limit. Satisfied the bag couldn't hold even one more urchin, she attached the float bag and began filling it with air. As the bag lifted free of the bottom, she waved goodbye to Garth and then gazed up toward the surface.

*   *   *   *   *

The door to Scott Chen's office was closed, muffling the clamor from downstairs where workers were processing yesterday's load of urchins. Chen leaned back in the swivel chair at his desk and rubbed his temple, holding the phone loosely to his ear. His wife's voice grated on his nerves, and he was anxious to end the conversation. He had tried to distract her by changing the subject, but she wasn't falling for it.

"This morning I go to the office to straighten up, and what do I find? More overdue bills!" she screeched into the phone. "What is going on? You talk about all this money coming in, but you haven't made the lease payment on the Oregon plant. Why? I ask you, why?"

"Please dear, do not concern yourself with these things. I will take care of it," Chen murmured, hoping to calm her down.

"When, I ask you? And when do you come home? You spend all your time at this new plant, never home anymore. What kind of life is this?"

Chen sighed. "You know I can't leave until we finish processing. Today is the last day of diving for this week. As soon as those urchins are processed and the trays are shipped out, then I will take time off. I promise."

"And then it will be a new week, and you'll be gone again. I don't understand why you wanted this second processing plant. We were doing just fine with the business here. Why do you overload yourself like this?"

"To make money, foolish woman," he said harshly, fed up with her tirade. Chen knew it was a mistake as soon as the words left his mouth.

"Foolish?" she shrieked. "You say I'm foolish? Have you forgotten where the money came from to start this business? It all came from me, Scott Chen, you ungrateful bastard. Before I met you, I worked ten hours a day and invested every penny."

"I'm sorry, dear. I shouldn't have said that."

She continued as though he hadn't apologized. "Without my money, there would be no business! What makes you think...."

Chen held the phone away from his ear, but could still hear her screaming. He finally interrupted, saying he had a call on another line.

"Sorry, I must go," he said, then pushed a button to cut off the connection and slammed the receiver down. Chen leaned back in the chair, closed his eyes and pressed his fingers against his temples, trying to stop his throbbing headache.

*   *   *   *   *

James Holt shoved aside the stack of reports he'd been working on and opened the file on Kessler. Locating Carl was clearly his first priority, but he had damn little to work with. Didn't even know the suspect's last name, much less what he looked like. All they really knew was that he hung around the Cap Sante Marina in Anacortes. Maybe they'd get lucky and come up with a match on the fingerprints.

Picking up the phone, Holt punched in the number for the lab, and after introducing himself, told the clerk what he needed, then waited on hold while she checked.

"I'm sorry sir, but I don't have any results for you yet," she informed him. "There's a heavy backlog, and we run the most urgent ones first."

"This is urgent, dammit." Holt listened for a moment and replied, "I don't care how it was marked when it came in. Those prints belong to a suspect in a homicide case. I need those results, and I need 'em yesterday."

"I'll see what I can do," the woman said politely, but with zero enthusiasm.

Holt broke the connection, then dialed the Kessler's number. He needed to speak with Sheri, let her know she could go ahead with funeral arrangements, but also explain that the boat would be tied up for awhile longer. It was still docked at Neah Bay's Coast Guard Station, and he wanted to keep it there for the time being.

"Hello," Sheri answered softly, sounding vulnerable.

Speaking gently, Holt summarized the results of the autopsy, but he couldn't think of a way to cushion the final conclusion. "The findings of the autopsy confirm what we suspected. There is no doubt, your husband was murdered, ma'am."

"I can't believe this," she protested. "Why?"

"We don't have any answers yet, but we're following up some leads. We found your husband's truck abandoned thirty miles west of Port Angeles, and right now, our number one priority is to locate Carl."

"He called here this morning."

"He what?" Holt said loudly, shocked at the announcement. "Why didn't you call me immediately?"

"I didn't think…I didn't know it was important."

Holt was stunned. Carl had disappeared the night her husband was murdered, and she didn't think it was important?

Sheri continued. "Carl sounded shocked when I told him George had been killed. He had no idea anything had happened. He said he hit a deer on the way out to Neah Bay and the engine overheated. It got so hot, he was afraid it would seize up or something, so he parked the truck and hitched a ride back to town."

"Did he say where he's been for the last three days?" Holt asked, trying to keep the sarcasm out of his voice.

"Well, yes. He felt bad about wrecking the truck and figured he'd blown his chance at a good job, so he went straight to a bar and started drinking. Said he'd been sober for over a year, but once he got started…he went on a binge and stayed drunk for days. This morning he was sober enough to realize that he was just making things worse and decided to call."

Holt's suspicious mind was working overtime, but he kept his thoughts to himself. "Did he happen to give you a phone number where he could be reached?"

"No, he didn't." Sheri's voice faltered. "I'm sorry…I didn't think to ask. He sounded so sincere—I just can't believe he had anything to do with George's death."

"We still need to locate him and ask him some questions. If he was at a bar that night, someone should be able to verify his presence." Holt doubted that would be the case, but he didn't say it out loud. He told

Sheri that a deputy would be in Anacortes the next day to drop off George's belongings, and that they might have a few more questions for her. "And Mrs. Kessler—if Carl should call again, I'd appreciate hearing from you immediately."

After hanging up, Holt stood and began pacing back and forth in front of his desk, replaying the conversation in his mind. The first time they'd talked, Sheri had told him she'd never met Carl, but listening to her now….there'd been, what? A sense of familiarity? It sounded like she was defending the guy. Holt kept coming back to the same question–why had Kessler been killed? Who would benefit from his death?

Holt returned to his chair and reached for his pipe. Watching the smoke drift toward the ceiling, he let his mind wander. There had to be a motive, and if he could just figure out what it was, he'd have his killer. An ugly thought came to mind, and he reached for the phone.

"Directory assistance, what city, please?"

He requested listings for all the insurance brokers in the Anacortes area, jotting them down as the operator reeled off names and numbers. Holt looked at the list of seven agents and dialed the first one. A female voice answered cheerfully, asking how she could help him.

Holt introduced himself and asked if the company carried any insurance policies on George Kessler.

A few minutes later, she came back on the line and said, "No, I'm sorry. We have nothing under that name."

After the fifth negative response, Holt figured he was wasting his time, but there were two more companies on his list, both located in the nearby city of Mount Vernon. He dialed a number and went through the routine again.

"Yes, we do happen to carry insurance for George Kessler. Why? Has there been an accident involving one of his vehicles?"

"As a matter of fact, there was, but that's not the reason I'm calling. I'd like to know if you carry life insurance on Mr. Kessler." Holt heard a sharp intake of breath before he was put on hold, and a couple of minutes passed before another voice came on the line.

"This is Bob Cranston. May I help you?"

Holt repeated his question regarding life insurance.

"Well, yes, we do have a policy on Mr. Kessler. I wrote it up myself. Must have been about two years ago. May I inquire why you're asking?"

Holt ignored the question. "What is the amount of the policy?" He unconsciously held his breath while he waited for an answer.

"He has excellent coverage. A quarter-million dollars—to be exact."

Holt exhaled quietly, not speaking for a few seconds while he absorbed the news. The phone line seemed to vibrate with the silence. He cleared his throat and told the insurance agent about Kessler's death, concluding from the shocked response that Sheri hadn't contacted him yet. After giving him a brief summary of the circumstances, he politely fended off the man's questions and ended the call.

There was no longer any question of who to send to Anacortes–Holt would handle this one personally. He wanted to be there to see the reaction on Sheri's face when he asked her about the insurance money. Tomorrow should prove to be an interesting day.

CHAPTER *Eighteen*

*L*ifting one of the plastic trays from the water, Scott Chen examined the roe. It was plump and firm, curling inward at the edges, with a nice golden color. The seepage of milky fluids indicated that the urchin had been ready to spawn, but the bath of salts and alum would dry that up, and the roe should bring a good price in Japan.

Chen frowned, thinking about the extra money he would have to pay out for today's urchins—thanks to that trouble-maker, Mickey Sutter. American women didn't know their place, and now, even his own wife had started sticking her nose in his business where it didn't belong, nagging him with her questions.

Mr. Kashimoto, the plant manager, stood near a row of tables, supervising the workers who scooped roe from the cracked urchin shells. Seeing Chen, he walked over to greet him.

"Urchins look very good today, yes?" he said, bowing his head slightly.

Chen had seen nothing to complain about, but he snapped at him rudely.

"This water is not cold enough! I want it checked immediately. And if you wish to keep your job, you will make sure the workers do not miss any more pieces of kelp when cleaning the roe."

Shocked at the rebuke, the manager stood speechless as Chen turned and stormed back to his office. At a nearby table, the employees cast their eyes downward and went back to work, pretending they hadn't heard anything.

Chen closed the door to his office and sank into his chair. In the quiet of the room, he heard the fax machine spit out a sheet of paper and reached for it, knowing it would be from his buyer. He scanned the page eagerly, looking for the numbers, and breathed a sigh of relief as he read them.

The amount of deposit was well over the one-hundred-fifty-thousand-dollars that he'd been expecting, and this was just for the urchins he'd bought from *Intruder*. Now he could pay off the bills and cover today's urchins, and hopefully it would get his wife off his back. When the money came in for the rest of this week's product, he would take a well-deserved bonus and buy stock in that company. His wife would not approve, of course, so he would tell her nothing.

The phone rang, jarring him from his thoughts.

"Chen Trading Company. This is Scott Chen," he said pleasantly.

"Mr. Chen, this is Officer Brad Sanders with the Department of Fish and Wildlife. I'd like to drop by and talk with you and wondered when would be a good time."

Chen's cheerful mood evaporated. "Today is not good. I am very busy."

"Mr. Chen, this won't take a great deal of time, but it is rather important."

"It is also important that I get to the bank before they close, which means I must leave soon." Chen had no desire to meet with Sanders, and he tried to brush him off. "Whatever it is you wish to speak about, it will have to wait for another time."

"Since you're in such a rush, Mr. Chen, I'll get right to the point. Your company was involved in a poaching operation at Neah Bay last week and charges will be brought against you. Poaching is a felony violation," Sanders said sharply. "However, if you cooperate with the investigation, the prosecutor will take that into consideration."

Chen gasped, his mind racing. How could this be happening? The urchins were long gone, and they couldn't possibly prove anything.

"This is ridiculous. I know nothing about any poaching. You make some kind of mistake."

"Mr. Chen, thirty totes with your name stamped on the side left the dock Saturday night, filled with illegal urchins."

"No, it cannot be. I know nothing of this. Someone else must have used my totes." Chen tried to swallow, but his mouth was too dry.

"If that's the way you want to play it, we can do this the hard way, Mr. Chen. But you might want to reconsider. You have no previous violations, and the prosecutor is willing to reduce the charge against you to a misdemeanor—but only if you cooperate. This is a one-time offer. No deals later on." Sanders glanced across the desk at the prosecutor who nodded in agreement.

Chen fought the urge to panic and struggled to think. It was obvious Sanders wanted him to make a deal. Maybe the fish cop didn't have any proof, and he was trying to trick him into confessing.

"I do not have to listen to these accusations," Chen said. "This is outrageous, and I have nothing more to say to you. You have more questions—you call my attorney."

"You'll regret that decision, Mr. Chen—I guarantee it," Sanders said in a soft, but ominous voice. "Have a nice day, Chen. You'll be hearing from us."

Chen heard a click and the line went dead. He hurled the phone across the room, and it crashed to the floor in a tangled heap. Kicking his chair out of the way, he began pacing back and forth behind the desk. Stopping suddenly, he stared down at the fax sheet on the desk and looked at the deposit amount again. His hard work was just starting to pay off, and now this call from Sanders.

"Nooo, this cannot be," he said in a low, agonized voice. He knew that he needed to get to the bank and transfer money into his account to cover the checks for today's urchins, but instead, he sat back down and stared at the fax.

If he could invest all that money in stocks, instead of paying stupid bills, he would be rich. Of course, then everyone would be looking for him. Bill collectors, urchin divers, even his own nagging wife. Why, he would have to....disappear. But, where could he go? He glanced at the clock and saw he could still make the bank if he hurried.

Chen made no move to get up. He needed to think.

CHAPTER *Nineteen*

*T*he *Intruder* was tied alongside the old fuel dock with a good-sized load of urchins on deck, and Tim ran the hoist, pulling on the davit arm until two bulging ring-nets were positioned above the cluster of empty bins.

Ted Drake stepped up close to read the scale. "Whoo-ha! Eight-hundred and sixty-two pounds. Gonna have me a fat paycheck tonight." He smiled and popped the cap on a Budweiser, tipped it back and guzzled half. Pulling a second beer from his coat pocket, he offered one to Tim. "Here, man, join the party."

Tim shook his head, leaning down to grab the drawstring on the bottom of a bag.

"Hey, we got reason to celebrate," Ted insisted, thrusting the beer at him. "Besides, I'm feelin' generous and this here's your bonus." He laughed at his own joke and took another swig from the bottle.

Ignoring him, Tim concentrated on dumping the urchins and moved to untie the second bag.

"Well, you're no fun," Ted said with a sneer. He downed the rest of his beer and tossed the empty on top of the urchins. "What'sa matter? Poor little Indian can't handle his liquor?" He uncapped another beer, took a long swig and belched loudly.

Standing downwind, Tim caught a whiff of his foul breath and grimaced. The guy was a disgusting pig. Tim was about ready to tell him so, but Ted had already turned away and stood gazing at the water beyond the boat. On the deck of *Intruder*, Steve leaned against the railing, watching Bart as he gathered the diving gear and stowed it in the lazaret. Ted grabbed the empty bottle from the tote and yelled down to Steve.

"Hey, Steve! Bet ya' twenty bucks you can't hit this with one shot." Ted slung the bottle out past the stern of the boat, and it landed with a splash, bobbing to the surface about forty feet away.

Steve glanced casually at the floating bottle, took a long pull from his whiskey flask, then slipped inside the cabin. A moment later, the barrel of a .22 pistol protruded from an open window on the far side of the boat. The gun made a loud crack, and a spout of water appeared near the bottle, a little high and off to the left.

Ted gave a hoot and slapped his leg. A rapid series of shots erupted from the cabin, raising tiny water spouts all around the target. Finally, the sixth bullet hit the mark and the bottle shattered with a loud pop.

Tim heard the gunshots over the sound of the winch and thought about telling them to knock it off, but decided he better keep his mouth shut. The Drake brothers were already half-plowed, and it probably wouldn't take much to set them off. They were a couple of assholes, and he wasn't sorry he'd talked to the fish cop. These guys deserved whatever they got, and with luck, he'd get to see them hauled off to jail. Tim glanced toward shore, wondering when it would all go down.

*   *   *   *   *

Leaving the pier after unloading, Rick Kautzman pushed forward on the throttles and *Rough Rider* surged ahead in the direction of the old fuel dock. He glanced again at the fish ticket and check lying on the dash, and a smile came over his face. Adding up his weight, he'd been disappointed to see it was under three thousand, but the price more than made up for it. His check from Pacific Fresh came to a little over four grand. When he called home this evening, he'd have good news for a change.

Troubled Waters

Approaching the dock, Rick spotted the fuel truck parked close to shore and switched on his fathometer to keep an eye on the depth. At low tide, this end of the bay was pretty shallow, and he didn't want to bang up one of his propellers. With the meter reading eight feet, he shifted into neutral and stepped outside as the boat coasted toward the pilings. He helped Chad tie up the boat, then climbed onto the dock.

"How ya doing?" Al greeted him. "Good day today?"

"I can't complain—now that we're getting a decent price for our urchins."

Al started pulling hose off the drum, and Rick gave him a hand, lowering the fuel nozzle over the side of the dock.

"Where's your hired help today?" Rick asked.

"Tim's running the hoist," Al said, nodding toward the end of the dock.

Rick nodded and looked in the direction he'd pointed. All he could see were empty bags being lowered from the hoist, but couldn't tell which boat it was below the edge of the dock. "Who's unloading?"

"*Intruder*," Al said with a dark scowl.

"I guess Chen must be matching the price," Rick commented.

"Well, the Drake brothers seem to be celebrating something. Gettin' drunk and shooting off a damn gun. More trouble than they're worth." Al looked down the length of the dock and spotted two figures walking toward them. "Speak of the devil."

As they came closer, Rick noticed the glowing cigarette dangling from Ted Drake's mouth. Al cursed under his breath—something about stupid idiots—then yelled at him to put the damn thing out.

Ted flipped the cigarette into the water and grinned back at him. "Don't sweat it, pops. Everything's cool."

Al glared at them as they passed, then looked toward the beach, scanning the parking area as though looking for something. With a slight shake of his head, he turned back to watch the fuel meter.

Rick sensed something odd about the motion, and it tweaked his curiosity. But the brooding look on Al's face stifled any questions, and he let it go for the time being.

*　　*　　*　　*　　*

Brad Sanders spoke into the phone, his voice tense with excitement.

"It's on, Chief. I've got a Coast Guard cutter standing by, and our ETA is ten minutes. I don't expect any trouble, but I'd like some men on the dock in case anyone tries to leave the vessel when we pull alongside."

"You've got it," said Makah Chief of Police, Ken McQuigan, adding, "I got a call from Al at the fuel dock ten minutes ago. He said the Drake brothers were drinking beer and throwing bottles in the water, then shooting at them with a pistol. I told him to let us handle it, so watch yourself when you go aboard."

"Thanks for the warning. We're on our way." Sanders cradled the receiver and walked briskly toward the door. Once out of the building, he broke into a trot and jogged down the long wooden dock to the waiting cutter. As soon as he stepped on board, two seamen cast off the lines, and the vessel backed rapidly out of its slip. As Sanders worked his way forward to the bridge, the vessel picked up speed, matching his own rush of excitement.

*　　*　　*　　*　　*

"OK, that's it," Al said, flipping a switch to shut off the pump.

Chad pulled the fuel nozzle from the flush opening on deck and hung on to it while Al began reeling in the hose. Stepping to the side of the boat, he twisted the end of the hose to take a kink out and felt his foot kick something. Chad heard it slide across the deck and looked down in dismay as the fuel cap skidded straight toward an open scupper. Helpless to stop it, he watched as the cap slid out the drain hole and fell into the water, making a plopping sound.

"Son-of-a-bitch!" he shouted.

Writing a check for the fuel, Rick heard the cussing and leaned over the edge of the dock to see Chad staring down into the water at the side of the boat.

Chad glanced up with a pained look. "You're gonna kill me."

"Why is that?" Rick didn't think he wanted to hear what was coming.

"I hit the fuel cap with my foot and it went straight out the scupper."

Rick let out a groan. He didn't have an extra one, and that meant he'd have to dive down and get it. The thought of putting his cold, damp wetsuit back on made him shudder, but he didn't have any choice.

"Break out my gear," he said with a sigh. "I'll see if I can find it. And you better grab my dive light, too. I'll probably need it." Rick turned around to see an amused smile on Al's face.

"Not funny," he said handing him the check. He pocketed the receipt and climbed back down on the boat, then disappeared inside the cabin to suit up.

*   *   *   *   *

Bart finished tying the last net and leaned it against the side of the boat. He still needed to stow all the nets and finish cleaning up the boat, but his hands ached with cold, and one of his knuckles throbbed where he'd been stabbed by an urchin spine. He blew on his hands to warm them and looked around at the mess. Streamers of kelp and broken urchin spines littered the deck, mixed with splatters of smashed roe. Screw it. He deserved a break.

Bart stepped inside the warm cabin and headed straight for the storage compartment where Steve kept his whiskey, fetched out a fresh bottle and took a long drink, feeling the warmth spread to his belly. After a few more shots, he felt much better and went outside to finish up.

A Coast Guard cutter came into view around the end of the pier just as Bart finished rinsing down the deck, and he wondered what they were up to. The cutter motored straight for the *Intruder*, and as it came alongside, two seamen jumped aboard with lines, while two men armed with M-16s watched from the railing.

Chief Petty Officer Carrick climbed aboard with his pistol drawn and gestured at Bart. "Hands above your head. Come on, get 'em up. Where's the rest of the crew?"

"What is this shit?" Bart said, reluctantly raising his hands. "They were just shootin' at bottles." Looking up at the dock, he saw two Makah policemen and asked, "What's the big deal?"

"Where are the others?" the Coast Guard Officer demanded tersely.

"They already split. Hey, man, I didn't have nothin' to do with it, alright? I just work for 'em." Bart noticed the fish cop standing by the door to the cabin and wondered why he was there. He found out soon enough.

"Bart Stacy, you're under arrest for a felony fisheries violation," Sanders announced, then read him his rights.

Stunned, Bart shook his head in disbelief and watched as a couple of seaman entered the cabin, their pistols drawn and ready.

"Hey, come on, man. This is all bullshit. I gotta put the boat on the mooring, and then I'm gonna have me a hot shower and get some grub."

"No, Bart, that's not happening. This vessel has been impounded, and you're going to jail." Sanders turned and looked up at Chief McQuigan. "Cuff him as soon as he gets up the ladder. I'll stop by after we get the boat moved and finish up the paperwork." He looked at Bart, who stood there with his mouth agape, and gestured toward the ladder. "Get moving."

*   *   *   *   *

By the time Rick surfaced near *Rough Rider's* stern, there was barely enough light to see Chad waiting for him on the dive platform. Rick handed up the dive light, grabbed the edge of the platform and gave a kick with his fins, boosting himself out of the water. He sat on the stern, pulled off his mask and fins, and passed them to Chad.

"Well? Did you find it?"

Rick didn't answer immediately. He climbed over the dive hose to stand in front of the engine room, dumped his weight belt on deck, then unhooked a small mesh bag from his harness. "I found all kinds of junk down there," he said finally. Reaching into the bag, he pulled out a pair of gold-rimmed glasses and handed them to Chad.

"But did you find the fuel cap?" Chad demanded, sounding worried.

"And I found these," Rick said, dragging out a pair of rusty wire cutters. "So, it wasn't a total waste of time."

"Ah, come on, you're torturing me."

"Wait, there's more." He pulled a tangled wad of hooks and fishing line from the bag and shook his head sadly. Rick managed to keep a straight face for a few seconds before breaking out in a grin, then reached into the bag and came out with the flat metal fitting that sealed the fuel port.

Chad closed his eyes and breathed a sigh of relief.

"Hey, you find your gas cap?" Al called down from the edge of the dock.

"Yeah, I got it," Rick said, looking up. "Found a pair of expensive looking glasses, too. Have you heard of anyone losing a pair? It doesn't look like they been down there long, and whoever it was might be glad to get 'em back."

"No, can't think of anyone right off. But I'll ask around."

"Here…why don't you take them. You're more likely to find the owner than I am," Rick said and climbed onto the roof of the cabin to pass them up.

Al tucked the glasses in his jacket pocket, then said casually, "Well, you sure missed all the action, fooling around with your night dive."

"What's that?"

"Coast Guard showed up with the fish cop and Makah Police and boarded the *Intruder*. Busted 'em for poaching." Al chuckled and his eyes twinkled merrily. "They impounded the boat and hauled Bart off to jail. Too bad the Drake brothers were already gone."

"No kidding! How did they catch them?"

"I don't know, but it couldn't happen to a nicer bunch."

"You just made my day." Rick laughed and climbed down off the cabin. "See you later," he said and waved to Al in the darkness before stepping inside the cabin. He was eager to change into his dry, warm clothes, but the shower would have to wait. They were already late for dinner at Mickey's, and he didn't want to miss out on his share of lasagna.

CHAPTER *Twenty*

*H*olding a fresh drink, Mickey eased herself into a chair in the living room and licked a bit of salt from the rim before taking a sip. She gazed across the room at Garth and Jerry, sitting on the rickety old couch, and hoped it wouldn't collapse under their weight.

"Did anybody see *Rough Rider* come in?" she asked.

"Yep, yep. They unloaded right before we did," Jerry answered, pulling on the end of his mustache. "Can't imagine what's holding him up. Must be taking the world's longest shower."

"He told me they had to get fuel," Mickey said, glancing at her watch. "But that shouldn't have taken this long."

"Don't know about anybody else, but I'm about to starve," Colin announced. He had turned a kitchen chair around backwards and sat with his elbows propped on the back. "How long are we going to wait?"

"We'll give 'em ten more minutes, and then we eat," Mickey answered.

"All right! That means more groceries for us," Colin said, patting his stomach.

Jerry reached into the sack at his feet and pulled out a can of Rainier ale, offering one to Colin and Garth.

"How can you drink that crap?" Colin responded, his face screwed up in disgust.

"Hey, it has character," Jerry said, taking a sip.

Garth laid his arm across the back of the couch and turned toward Jerry. "What was Jimmy Lee's reaction when he heard the price?"

"He did plenty of whining, of course, but he paid. That's all I care about."

"Bruce Engals sure threw a fit when he found out most of his boats were selling to Pacific," Garth said, slapping his knee. "He tried threatening the new buyer, but Hansen's man was cool—he just ignored him."

Jerry laughed. "Yeah, it was great. I thought Engals would blow a gasket, his face was so red."

Mickey nodded, smiling. "When I went inside to get my fish ticket, he made some rude comments, and I told him if he kept it up, Colin would toss him in the drink. He left me alone after that." Her eyes sparkled and she started to say something else, but was interrupted by a knock at the door.

Rick and Chad apologized for being late, but no one paid attention. The kitchen table was laid out with two loaves of garlic bread, a huge pan of lasagna and a heaping bowl of salad, and they all swarmed around as though they hadn't eaten for days. Dishing up his plate, Rick told the story of the lost fuel cap, and Chad, standing beside him, looked like he wanted to change the subject.

"Ten feet of water!?" Jerry exclaimed. "Why didn't you strip down and dive in bare-assed? You would've been done in two minutes flat."

Rick laughed and shook his head. "Next time, I'll call you—let you demonstrate."

"Hey, there won't be any next time," Chad protested.

Plates piled high, they crowded into the living room and attacked the food with serious intent. No one spoke for several minutes, except to compliment Mickey's cooking. When Rick finished his plate, he went back for seconds, followed by Colin and Garth.

Mickey was amazed at how much food Rick could put away and never gain any weight. He ate more than Garth, who probably outweighed him by a hundred pounds. Colin was the same way, and she wondered where they put it all.

Pushing his plate away, Jerry leaned back and gave a contented groan, then launched into a story about the time he dropped his favorite pocket knife overboard in twenty feet of water. Claimed he dove in buck naked and swam down to get it.

Forty-degree water without a wetsuit? Mickey shivered at the thought. No way! She'd either suit up or buy herself a new knife.

"Did you guys hear the news about *Intruder*?" Rick asked.

"What's that? Did they sink?" Garth asked, sounding hopeful.

"No, but they got busted for poaching, and their boat was impounded."

Colin and Garth cheered, and everyone began talking at once. Mickey sat quietly, feeling a warm glow of satisfaction and smiled broadly as the others bombarded Rick with questions.

"I don't know how it all came about," Rick said finally. "But I have a hunch Al knows something he wasn't telling me." He turned his gaze on Mickey and asked, "Do you know how they got caught?"

The question caught Mickey by surprise, and she was grateful for a mouthful of food, giving her time to think. She made a big production out of swallowing before responding.

"Well…as a matter of fact, I might." Mickey grinned impishly, enjoying the agitated look on Rick's face. "I found some fresh urchin spines on the dock the day before the season started. I reported it, but I didn't think anything would come of it. Sanders made it sound like there wasn't enough evidence."

Rick looked questioningly at Colin, but he just smiled and shrugged.

"Well, I'm glad they caught the bastards," Garth said.

Mickey nodded. "Me, too. It really pisses me off that those guys have been getting away with robbery, while the rest of us struggle to make an honest living." She was dying to tell the rest of the story, but she'd promised Al to keep quiet about Tim's part in it. Seeing the inquisitive look in Rick's eye, she decided it was time to change the subject.

"Anyone want to get beat in a game of cribbage?" she asked.

"I feel pretty lucky tonight," Garth said, accepting the challenge.

"Loser gets to help with the dishes," she warned him.

"Hope you don't mind getting your hands wet," he said with a grin as Mickey went to fetch the cribbage board.

*   *   *   *   *

Sitting on the hard lumpy mattress, Bart stared unseeingly at the brick wall opposite his bunk. The walls were painted blue, and a single bulb on the ceiling, encased in a wire cage, bathed the tiny cell in bright, harsh light. The hallway was visible through the barred door, but no one had come or gone for over two hours, so he'd quit looking. His jeans were stiff and crusty with salt, covered with red stains from urchin shells, and he wanted a shower. But not half as bad as he wanted a damn drink. They hadn't let him take anything off the boat. His money was still there, stuffed down inside a tennis shoe at the bottom of his duffel. Lot of good it did him now. They let him make one phone call before locking him up, but he'd gotten the answering machine at Steve's girl-friend's place and there was no telling when they'd get his message. Probably out partying somewhere, he thought sourly.

Bart heard the muffled sound of voices and footsteps coming down the hall, and then the groaning squeak of metal as the door to his cell opened. He kept his eyes on the wall, not wanting to seem anxious. Brad Sanders stepped inside, telling the jailor he'd yell when he was ready to leave. The door clanged shut, and Sanders stood there, silently watching him.

"What the hell you staring at?" Bart asked defiantly.

"You're in a lot of trouble Bart. Maybe you'd like to talk about it."

"I don't have anything to say—not to you. This is all bullshit, man, and I know better than to spill my guts to a cop." Bart slid back and leaned against the wall, putting his boots up on the edge of the bunk. "You think I'm stupid, or what?"

Sanders tucked a wad of snuff under his lip before speaking. "I think you been keeping some bad company, Bart, and I don't think you can afford any more mistakes. You already have three misdemeanor convictions—drunk driving, shoplifting and possession of marijuana—and I think the judge will take that into account when he sentences you on this felony."

"Hey, man, you don't scare me. I ain't going down for no felony." Bart smiled confidently, puffing himself up. "Steve and Ted got the best lawyers in the business, and they been through all this shit before. They'll get us off—you wait and see."

Sanders snorted in disbelief, then responded in a hard voice.

"You really believe they'll pay for your attorney? If you think they give a shit about you, then you are stupid. Where are your good buddies right now?" Sanders paused and gave him a pitying look. "Get real, Bart. You're just a grunt. You wait on those guys hand and foot, clean up after 'em, even park their damned boat for 'em. They pay you a tiny fraction of the money, and you probably get cheated on that score, too."

Bart scowled at the floor, not saying anything. With his sunburned face and long hair ratted by the wind, he looked tired and forlorn.

"They're not your friends, Bart," Sanders said calmly. "They're out partying while you sit here in jail, and when they find out….well, they'll be worrying about themselves. The Drake brothers couldn't care less what happens to you."

"You're just saying that to turn me against 'em. They'll post bail and get me out of here—I know they will. Our attorney will get a court order to release the boat, and we'll be back to work in no time."

Sanders just stared at him, shaking his head slowly from side to side, then signaled the jailor that he was ready to leave. As the door clanged shut behind him, he turned to look at Bart through the bars.

"A Deputy Sheriff will be here tomorrow to transport you to the county jail in Port Angeles where you'll be arraigned. We'll see how fast your buddies come to the rescue then. But if I were you, Bart, I'd be thinking about who else I could call."

*   *   *   *   *

"Fifteen-two, fifteen-four and eight are twelve. I'm out," Mickey said gleefully.

"Aarrgghhh…and I was so close." Garth threw his cards down on the couch and stretched his arms above his head. "Guess I better go see if Colin needs help with those dishes." He smiled ruefully, stood up and lumbered into the kitchen.

Jerry's mouth opened in a huge yawn. "Guess it's time for me to hit the rack."

Rick and Chad nodded in agreement. As they rose to their feet, a loud whoop and holler erupted from the kitchen, catching everyone's attention.

"Come here, come here! You guys aren't gonna believe this," Garth yelled. They crowded around the sink to see what had him so excited.

"He's been scrubbing and scrubbing…but….he can't get all the black out…." Garth shook with laughter, unable to talk anymore, so he just pointed.

Colin stood with his hands in the sink, holding the lasagna pan and a wad of coarse steel wool. He looked totally bewildered by the sudden attention. "What? I'm just trying to get this pan clean. This black shit is really hard to get out."

Mickey peered over his shoulder and grimaced. "Colin. That's my brand new Teflon pan. That black shit is the non-stick coating, you dumbshit."

Colin closed his eyes and winced. "You mean…?"

Mickey's answer was drowned out by laughter.

"You better go get yourself some glasses, Colin," Garth teased, cuffing him lightly on the shoulder.

"Hey, I found a nice pair underwater when I dove for my fuel cap," Rick chimed in. "Make you a good deal on them."

Colin had heard enough razzing and ran everyone out of the kitchen. Mickey walked them to the door and said goodnight as they filtered out.

Rick was last to leave, and he paused at the door to zip up his parka. "Why do I have the feeling you know more about the Drake episode than you're letting on?"

"I'm sworn to secrecy, and it's killing me, so please don't ask. I'll give you the full story later on. I promise."

He frowned and shook his head. "Do the Drakes brothers know you're the one who reported the urchin spines?"

Now it was Mickey's turn to frown, recalling the note she'd found on the boat. "Yeah, I'm pretty sure they do," she admitted reluctantly. "But hopefully, they'll be in jail soon and stay there long enough to forget."

"Please be careful, would you? I know you've got Colin around, but still—some of these guys play rough and you don't want to mess with them."

"You saying I shouldn't have turned them in? You would've done the same thing."

"Yeah, and I'm glad they got busted. I just want you to watch your back, okay?" He reached for the doorknob, then added, "Say, if you hear of anybody who lost a pair of glasses, I left them with Al. He was going to ask around, see if maybe one of the fisherman lost 'em."

"I thought you were kidding about that, just teasing Colin."

"No, they're for real. Nice gold-rimmed frames. I was trying to remember who had a pair like that, but…it's not coming to me. It's been a long day."

Mickey agreed, and they finally said goodnight. She closed the door gently and stood there for a moment, trying to pin down a thought that hovered just beyond reach. Too tired to think straight, she gave up and switched off the lights and headed for bed.

CHAPTER *Twenty-One*

*D*eputy Coroner James Holt was on the road by quarter to six Thursday morning, giving himself extra time to make the first ferry from Port Townsend to Whidbey Island. The boat left the dock at seven, and he didn't want to miss it.

It was just starting to get light, but the sunrise was hidden by a layer of dark, heavy clouds. Dirty spray splattered the windshield as a logging truck roared past in the opposite direction, and Holt flipped on the wipers. Setting the cruise control at sixty, he braced the steering wheel with his knee while pouring a cup of coffee from his thermos. He was glad he'd taken his own car. The big Pontiac sedan had plenty of leg room and a smooth quiet ride. Early morning traffic was light, and he relaxed behind the wheel, ignoring the scenery as he focused his mind on the day ahead.

As soon as he arrived in Anacortes, Holt planned to call on Mrs. Kessler. Now that he'd found the missing link, the pieces were falling neatly into place, and he was anxious to question her. Holt recalled his first murder investigation and the advice of the crusty old detective in charge. "Follow the money," he'd always said.

Well, the money trail had certainly provided him with a suspect in this case. A quarter-million-dollars was a powerful motive for murder. But still, something didn't feel right. Maybe it just seemed too easy.

Holt had been over it a hundred times and it was the only thing that made sense. It had seemed strange that Sheri hadn't known Carl's last name and then, when he disappeared with the truck right after George was killed, she doesn't even notify the police that he called. Holt hadn't found any evidence to suggest an unhappy marriage, but then he hadn't been looking. He would have to interview more of their friends and see if anything turned up.

Holt felt certain he would know more by the end of the day, but he still couldn't erase that nagging feeling of doubt. Letting out a sigh, he reached for his coffee.

*   *   *   *   *

Scott Chen woke up with a killer headache and a bad case of cotton mouth. He covered his face with a tangled corner of sheet and tried to go back to sleep, but thirst drove him from bed and he staggered into the bathroom. Filling the small plastic cup at the sink, he downed several glasses of water. The cool water felt good going down, but when it hit his stomach, he suddenly felt queasy. Chen squatted by the toilet, choking back the taste of bile in his throat. Moaning softly, he cradled his head in his hands and waited for his stomach to settle down.

He remembered going into the lounge for a quick drink before dinner, and then ordering another. After three or four, the rest of the evening was a blur, and Chen couldn't recall whether he'd eaten or not. How could he be so stupid? He needed to think his way out of this mess, but instead he'd gotten himself drunk. Now, he was paying for it with a head that felt like it might split in two.

Chen couldn't believe how fast everything was going wrong for him, and it couldn't be happening at a worse time—just when he was about to receive his reward for all the years of sacrifice and hard work. Now, he saw nothing but problems ahead. Still, there had to be something he could do.

Chen forced himself up, turned on the shower full blast and stripped off the rest of his clothes. His head roared with pain as he bent over the sink to brush his teeth, and he clung to the edge of the counter to steady himself. Checking his face in the mirror, he surveyed the bloodshot eyes and gray color. He wished he could go back to bed, forget about his problems for the time being, and sleep for another four hours. But, that wasn't going to help. Stepping into the shower, he stood under the scalding spray until his skin was bright pink and his headache had eased to a dull throb. After dressing, he rode the elevator down to the hotel lobby and took a booth in the coffee shop.

Chen was glad to see that the place was nearly deserted, hoping the service would be quick. The waitress brought him a plate of scrambled eggs and toast, and he forced himself to eat everything. By his third cup of coffee, he felt much better and began to think he might live. His mind was still fuzzy, but at least he could concentrate. Chen flashed on the money deposited in his international account and realized that he'd never made it to the bank to transfer any funds. The checks for yesterday's urchins would bounce when the divers tried to cash them—unless he was at the bank when it opened and covered things. But that wasn't his biggest concern.

It was that meddlesome fish cop, Sanders, sniffing around for evidence that he bought those illegal urchins. How could he possibly prove anything? The Drake brothers would never talk. They'd deny the whole thing and let their attorney deal with it. Besides, if Sanders had anything more than suspicion, wouldn't he have shown up with a warrant? The man was probably just bluffing, hoping to catch Chen off guard. He should put it out of his mind and go on with his business.

The waitress topped off his coffee and left the check, but Chen barely noticed, thinking back on his conversation with Sanders. His voice had sounded so arrogant, and the quietly spoken threat bothered Chen more than he wanted to admit. Easy to say there was nothing to worry about, but not so easy to believe it. He'd never been in trouble for anything more serious than a traffic ticket, and the thought of prison terrified him. He'd heard stories.

Troubled Waters

Chen shuddered and wiped a thin film of perspiration from his brow. He was so close. All he needed was a few more days, and he'd be rich. The money for the last few shipments of urchin roe would be wired to his account as soon as the product arrived in Japan. The market was holding strong and the exchange rate still favored the dollar. Even if the price dropped slightly, he could expect a very large sum—nearly half-a-million. Chen sucked in his breath, realizing it was more than enough to make a new start.

There were other ways to make money in the world besides processing urchins, especially for someone who was clever with his investments. The more Chen thought about it, the more it appealed to him. He might never have to work again. And the best part was—after getting rid of his nagging wife—all the money would be his.

Feeling energized, Chen laid down a ten dollar bill and headed for his car. With some careful planning, he could pull this off. He must show up at the plant like normal, and when the divers called about their checks, stall them. Tell them the bank had credited the money to the wrong account. Then tomorrow morning, deliver the last shipment of roe to the airport himself. After that, he would simply hide out until the money came through and leave the country. But where would he go? Not to worry. In a few days, his choices would be unlimited.

*   *   *   *   *

Bart lay on the bunk with a thin blanket pulled up over his chest. He'd taken off his rubber boots, but he still wore the same dirty work clothes, and there were dark rings beneath his eyes.

"Still here, huh, Bart?" Sanders asked him through the bars.

"What do you want?" he said, glaring up at Sanders.

"Just thought I'd see if you'd changed your mind about things." Sanders grinned at him. "Sometimes a good night's sleep gives a person a whole new outlook."

"Go to hell." Bart rubbed his face with both hands and sat up. He ran his tongue over his teeth, and his face twisted into a scowl. "How does a person go about gettin' a cup of coffee in this dump?"

"Try asking politely."

"Kiss my ass. I don't beg for nothin'."

Sanders turned to leave, then stopped and said casually, "Oh, by the way. You might be interested to know that Steve and Ted were arrested last night, but their attorney showed up first thing this morning and posted bail. They're back out on the street, probably having steak and eggs for breakfast, and here you sit."

Bart jumped to his feet and slung the blanket at Sanders. "That's a lie! You're just sayin' that. They wouldn't leave me in here."

Sanders smiled. "That's exactly what they've done. I checked with their attorney, and his secretary informed me that Steve and Ted made no arrangements on your behalf. She suggested you call a public defender."

Bart went into a rage. He heaved the mattress pad against the wall and pounded it with his fists, cursing at the top of his lungs. Sanders could still hear him at the far end of the hall as he entered McQuigan's office and closed the door.

"Let's give him time to calm down, then bring him out and give him a cup of coffee. If he wants confirmation, I'll let him call the attorney's office and hear it for himself." Sanders sat down in a chair and grinned. "I almost feel sorry for the guy."

Chief McQuigan nodded. "You've got about three hours before a deputy arrives to pick him up. Think he'll talk?"

Sanders leaned back in the chair. "Oh, yeah, I'm sure of it."

CHAPTER *Twenty-Two*

*H*olt kept an eye on the speedometer as he drove through downtown Anacortes, heading toward a residential area on the north side of town. He felt the car rock slightly as a gust of wind swept between the buildings, picking up leaves and trash from the gutter and swirling them along in its wake. It was a dark, cold miserable morning, and there were few people on the streets. Holt paid little attention to the tall, lanky man who hurried down the sidewalk, thin coat pulled tightly about his shoulders.

Stopping in front of a cafe, the man pulled a folded section of newspaper from his pocket and checked the notice again: AA Meeting, Thursday mornings at 9:00 in the banquet room of Mom's Restaurant. Across the street at the bank, a digital sign flashed forty-two degrees, then displayed the time—9:04. Inside his scuffed leather cowboy boots, the man's toes were already numb, and he shivered as the cold wind plucked at his collar and penetrated the thin cloth of his worn-out jeans. He still wasn't sure he wanted to do this, but at least it would be warm inside.

The restaurant was nearly empty, and the waitress at the counter looked up from her coffee and newspaper and directed him to a room in the back. The meeting hadn't started yet, and a small group of people were gathered around a long banquet table, chatting quietly. They all seemed to know each other, and the man was tempted to leave, but before he could move, a plump woman with brunette hair looked his way and waved to him with a friendly smile. Catching a whiff of coffee and cinnamon rolls, he decided to stay.

The meeting started with the Serenity Prayer, spoken by a gray-haired Native American named Bob. When he finished the prayer, everyone introduced themselves, with the brunette woman last in line before himself.

"My name is Marie, and I'm an alcoholic," she stated matter-of-factly. "I've been sober for eighteen months now, and I have some good news to share. The phone company called me in for my second interview last Tuesday, and they told me I got the job." She nodded happily as the others congratulated her, then turned his way, waiting for him to speak.

"My name is Carl," he began in a strained voice. "And I'm an alcoholic. I was sober for almost three years. But something bad happened a few days ago, and….I started up again." He fell silent, his weathered face etched with deep lines as he stared down at his calloused hands folded tightly around the coffee cup. His blue eyes were sad, and forty-five years of hard living made him look older than he was.

Marie thought he was attractive in a rugged sort of way, but his mustache and sandy brown hair were in bad need of a trim. She leaned toward him, her face filled with compassion, and prompted him to continue.

"Maybe it would help if you shared it with us. Just tell us what happened. Sometimes it's good to get things off your chest."

The silence stretched on. Finally, he cleared his throat and spoke. "I'm not sure where to start. Things were just starting to look up for me. And now, I think I'm in trouble…serious trouble."

*　　　*　　　*　　　*　　　*

The Kessler's living room was tastefully decorated in subtle shades of beige and bamboo green, and a three-panel room divider near the front door was painted with oriental landscapes. Holt was seated at the opposite end of the sofa from Sheri, and the bag containing George's belongings sat on the cushion between them. Silent tears ran down her cheeks as she reached inside the bag and pulled out the shirt George had been wearing when he died. Holt felt uncomfortable. He'd been so eager to question her, but now he was reluctant to begin.

Sheri wiped her eyes with her sleeve, stood up and left the room. While he was alone, Holt picked at the bag, sifting idly through the contents. A smaller bag inside held a gold wedding band, wallet, watch, some loose coins and the business card that had been found in George's shirt pocket. The card, from Fish and Wildlife Officer Brad Sanders, had a phone number scribbled on the back. When Sheri came back into the room, Holt dropped the card inside the bag and pushed it closed.

It had only been a few minutes, but she seemed to have regained her composure—no sign of tears on her freshly scrubbed face. She'd added a touch of eyeshadow, and her blond hair was now pulled back in a pony-tail and tied with a scarf that matched her powder blue sweat suit. Her eyes were a startling shade of green, and she looked at him with unexpected intensity.

"Is that it?" she asked pointing at the bag. "What about his things from the boat?"

Holt was surprised by her assertive tone, a dramatic change from the quiet tears just minutes before. He shifted his bulk on the sofa and leaned forward, resting his hands on his knees.

"The boat is being treated as a crime scene, and we need to preserve everything until we've gathered all the evidence. It's hard to know what might be important until we have a better picture of what happened." Holt watched Sheri closely while he spoke, looking for a reaction. "The boat and everything on board will be released eventually, but I can't say exactly when. That will depend on how soon we catch your husband's killer."

Sheri started to say something, then stopped abruptly. Arms folded across her chest, she massaged an elbow with one hand and stared off into space with a faraway look. A moment later, she asked him if he'd like a cup of coffee and, without waiting for an answer, got up and left the room. Holt followed her into the kitchen and watched as she busied herself making coffee. She was fashion-model thin with slender wrists and long manicured nails painted a frosty blue. She looked fragile, but he sensed a toughness beneath the delicate exterior.

Sheri asked if he wanted cream or sugar as she set two steaming mugs on the kitchen table, then took a seat across from him. Her eyes roamed the kitchen for a minute before focusing on Holt with undisguised anger.

"All you've told me so far is that my husband was murdered. I have a right to know what's going on. What is happening with your investigation? Do you have any leads? Do you have any suspects? Tell me what's happening."

Holt gazed at Sheri while he debated how to respond. She kept surprising him with her sudden mood swings, and he wasn't sure how to read her.

"We don't have all the answers yet, but I can tell you this much. Your husband arrived in Neah Bay sometime after one a.m. Sunday morning. We assume he pulled in at one of the docks and was coming up a ladder when he was struck on the side of the head with a wooden object. He must have fallen backwards onto the deck of the boat, fracturing his skull, and he died from internal bleeding. What we don't know is who knocked him off that ladder, and why." Holt watched Sheri closely, and his voice became hard. "Can you think of anyone who might have had a reason to kill your husband, Mrs. Kessler?"

Sheri shook her head slowly from side to side, staring blindly at the floor.

Holt pressed on, ignoring his conscience. He had to know.

"The person who killed your husband tried to make it look like an accident, and it almost worked. A few wood splinters that couldn't be explained made all the difference on the coroner's decision to do an autopsy. If we'd missed them, it would have been written off as an unfortunate accident." Holt placed both hands on the kitchen table and came up out of his chair, towering over her.

"Mrs. Kessler, I'm a little confused about something. You told me you never met this man Carl. Yet, you're the one he calls to explain why he never made it to Neah Bay. Carl goes missing the night your husband was murdered, and you don't call me the minute you hear from him. Would you like to explain that?"

"I already told you. Carl called to leave a message for George, telling him what happened to the truck."

"Yes, but that still doesn't explain why you didn't call me. You waited until I brought up Carl's name, and then, when you finally told me about his phone call, it sounded like you were defending the man." Holt paused and took a deep breath, then continued in a voice edged with steel.

"I keep asking myself who would benefit from your husband's death. And I only come up with one name, Mrs. Kessler. Your husband was insured for a quarter-million dollars—and you are the sole beneficiary. How much money did you promise Carl for killing your husband?"

Sheri looked stunned. It took several seconds for the full impact of the question to register, and her expression of disbelief quickly changed to horror. Unable to speak, she shook her head violently and sprang to her feet, sobbing loudly as she ran from the room.

As Holt started after her, the phone began ringing. Pausing by the phone in the kitchen, he cursed the rotten timing and debated whether to answer it. Hearing that Sheri had already picked it up, he gently lifted the extension and held it to his ear.

*   *   *   *   *

Listening to the phone ring for the fourth time, Mickey wondered if maybe her imagination was just working overtime, but she couldn't quit thinking about it. She was sure George wasn't wearing his glasses when they found him. So, where were they? Had they turned up somewhere on the boat? Ever since Rick mentioned finding a pair of glasses by the fuel dock, she'd been haunted by a growing suspicion. Just as Mickey was about to hang up, Sheri answered with a quiet hello.

"Hi, Sheri, this is Mickey. How are you holding up there, lady?"

Her reply came out in a sob, and Mickey couldn't understand anything she said.

"Sheri, what's the matter? Tell me what's wrong."

"I just can't believe it. He thinks that I murdered…" Her voice dissolved in another burst of crying.

"He thinks what? Who are you talking about?"

"That detective named Holt. He just accused me of having George murdered for the insurance money. How could he say that? I loved George," she said, her voice trailing off to a whisper.

"Aaahhh…man. Sheri, listen to me. That is the stupidest thing I've ever heard. The son-of-a-bitch is just doing his job, but he's not doing it very well by the sound of things. Don't let him get to you."

Sheri broke in, still sniffling noticeably, but no longer sobbing. "He's still here. In the other room."

"Well, you just tell him to leave. Is there anybody nearby who can come over right away and stay with you for a little while?"

"I could call my mom."

"Do that as soon as we hang up. You should have someone there with you. Sheri, I'm sorry to bother you with this right now—but I have one question. It might not be important, but….were George's glasses returned with his belongings?"

Sheri was quiet for a second. "I just went through his things and…no, his glasses weren't there. Why do you ask?"

"I'm not sure yet, but one of the divers found a pair of glasses under-water near the fuel dock, and I think they may be his." Mickey's mind was racing, and the pieces fell into place as she spoke. "If they are....it could be that George stumbled onto a poaching operation when he pulled into Neah Bay that night."

"Poaching? What are you talking about?"

"I may be jumping to conclusions here, so don't take this to heart. But, Brad Sanders just arrested some divers for poaching, and we know they were unloading their urchins at the fuel dock the night George arrived. If those really are his glasses, there's a good chance it all ties together somehow."

"Mickey, who are these divers? Who would kill for a bunch of lousy urchins?"

"Not for urchins, Sheri—for money. This business is full of greedy creeps, and the Drake brothers are the worst. This is only speculation on my part, but I'll let you know if I find out anything else."

Catching sight of Colin coming out of the motel, Mickey told Sheri she needed to go and reminded her to call her mom before hanging up.

*   *   *   *   *

Listening in on their conversation, Holt was about to interrupt when Mickey suddenly broke it off. He heard the click and knew she was gone. Burning with anger, he replaced the receiver and thought about what he'd just heard. Mickey's comments about him doing a lousy job really stung, and Holt felt like he'd been blindsided. He knew absolutely nothing about a poaching operation. What in what in the hell was going on? Recalling her reference to Brad Sanders, Holt knew who he intended to ask.

CHAPTER *Twenty-Three*

*I*n the banquet room of Mom's Restaurant, Carl had everyone's full attention. He paused for a drink of coffee to sooth his throat and found it had become cold while he talked.

"I know it looks bad…but you've got to believe me. I was worried he'd be mad at me for wrecking his truck, so I hid in a bottle for three days, not wantin' to face him. Hell, I didn't even know he'd been killed, not 'til yesterday when I called his wife. It shocked the hell out of me." He rubbed his forehead roughly with both hands and muttered hoarsely, "Christ, I've made a mess of things, and I don't know what the hell to do. I guess that's why I'm here."

It was nearly a full minute before anyone spoke.

"Carl," Marie said gently, breaking the silence. "You need to go to the police and tell them exactly what happened."

He looked up and saw the others nodding in agreement.

"But, what if they don't believe me?"

"You really don't have any choice," Bob said. "The police will be looking for you. But, if you turn yourself in, they'll be much more inclined to believe your story. Put your trust in a higher power. If you speak the truth, it will all work out."

"If I speak the truth…." Carl looked around the table, examining their faces. "Do you people believe me?"

At the far end of the table, James adjusted his tie before speaking. "It doesn't matter if we believe you or not. The police will find witnesses to back up your story, but as long as you avoid talking to them—it makes you look guilty as sin."

Carl leaned back and closed his eyes. His past experience with cops had never been pleasant, and that was all petty stuff compared to this. The thought of being a suspect in George's murder terrified him. He exhaled loudly before finally speaking.

"I guess you're right," he mumbled. "I'll take your advice." Carl slid back his chair and nodded at Marie. "Thank you for listening," he said, then headed for the door.

*   *   *   *   *

Mickey bounded up the concrete steps at the fuel depot and rushed into the office. Hearing the door creak, Al looked over to see who had come in.

"Well, well…how ya' doing, Sunshine? Surprised to see you hanging around during the closure. And don't try telling me you love Neah Bay that much."

"Not a chance," Mickey replied smiling. "We take turns keeping an eye on the boats, and I volunteered to stick around this time. I'm on my way to Port Angeles to run some errands, but I wanted to ask you about those glasses Rick found by the dock last night. Do you still have them?"

Al rubbed his chin and gave Mickey a curious look. "Yes, ma'am, I do. Haven't had a chance to ask anyone if they lost 'em. But, why in devil's name are you asking? I know you don't wear glasses."

"I think they belonged to George Kessler," she stated simply.

Al looked troubled, but he reached under the counter for the glasses and gave them to her. Mickey's hands trembled as she held the pair of gold-rimmed glasses out in front of her.

"I think they're his."

"You've lost me," Al said, looking perplexed. "If they're his, how did they end up in the water beside my dock?"

Mickey took a deep breath and blurted out her suspicions.

"I think George pulled into the bay while *Intruder* was offloading urchins and caught them red-handed. George hated poachers as much as I do, and if he saw something going on, he would've tried to stop them somehow."

"Whoa! Hold on a minute here. I thought George's death was an accident?"

Mickey glanced out the window at the fuel dock, her face grim. "It turns out that someone just wanted it to look that way. It never made sense to me that George would open his fishhold in the middle of the night, and there are other things that bothered me. Like shutting down his engine and turning off the depth sounder when his boat wasn't even anchored. I'll tell you one thing—if the Drake brothers are responsible for George's death, I want them to pay for it. Big time."

"I can see where you're headed with this, Missy. But, you don't even know for sure if these are George's glasses."

"George wasn't wearing his glasses when we found his body, and they weren't anywhere in sight on the boat, so I called Sheri before coming over here and asked if his glasses were returned with his personal belongings. She said they weren't."

"It's sounding more and more like something the police should be handling," Al cautioned.

Mickey snorted with disgust. "Yeah, well apparently they're too busy harassing the grieving widow. That son-of-a-bitch Holt was at Sheri's house when I called, and he had just accused her of hiring someone to kill George so she could collect the life insurance money."

"How much was he insured for?"

"It doesn't matter," she sputtered angrily. "The whole idea is totally absurd. Those two were madly in love."

"Maybe he cheated on her," Al suggested.

"Don't start," Mickey said, glaring at him. "It wasn't like that."

"Okay, okay, I was just playing devil's advocate. Don't get all worked up over it."

Mickey wasn't quite ready to drop the subject. "Holt got that crazy idea because Carl, the guy who was supposed to work on George's boat, never showed up. He just seemed to disappear. The point I'm trying to make is that Holt's looking for a murder suspect. That means he knows George's death wasn't an accident."

"What do you know about this guy, Carl? It does seem pretty suspicious that he disappeared the night George was killed. Maybe they got in a fight over something. Maybe he intended to steal George's boat and head for Hawaii. Who knows?"

Mickey stopped to consider it. "I've never met the guy, so I can't vouch for him. But it still seems like too much of a coincidence that the Drake brothers were offloading urchins around the time George would've gotten here."

Al still looked doubtful. "There's one major problem with your theory. If George caught them here at this dock and they had some kind of confrontation, how come Tim didn't mention it?"

Mickey had forgotten about Tim. "I don't know. Maybe he was too scared."

"Tim would have no part in covering up a murder," Al said.

Mickey wasn't so sure, but she kept her thoughts to herself.

"So, now what?" he asked. "You gonna share your suspicion with the cops?"

"That's where I'm headed, and when I drop these glasses off, I intend to tell Mr. Holt what I think really happened. Sheri has enough grief to deal with as it is, without him accusing her of murder. I'll try to reach Sanders, too, and see if maybe he can put some pressure on the Drake brothers while they're still in jail."

"Too late for that. Sanders called me earlier, said they were picked up last night, but their lawyer showed up first thing this morning. Steve and Ted are already out, and they're going to be wondering how they got caught." Al puffed on his cigarette and frowned through a cloud of smoke. "Sanders asked me to warn Tim, tell him to be on guard in case they suspect anything. You should be careful yourself, Missy."

She nodded, her face serious. "Don't worry, I'll be careful. But I just can't stand the idea of somebody getting away with murder. If I come up with anything else, I'll turn it over to the cops." Picking up the glasses, Mickey tucked them inside her backpack, hooked a strap over one shoulder, and flashed Al a reassuring smile as she slipped out the door.

Back at the motel, she put in a call to Sanders.

"Highway Patrol," a female dispatcher answered crisply.

"My name is Mickey Sutter, and I need to get a message to Fish and Wildlife Officer Brad Sanders, right away."

"Are you calling about a violation in progress?"

"No, but it involves a case he's working on, and it's really important that I speak with him as soon as possible."

"He's out in the field right now, but I'll give him your message the next time he calls in. Is there a number where you can be reached?"

Mickey said she'd try again later and hung up. Heading back to the room, she thought about Steve Drake being out on bail. It was probably all a big joke to him, the arrogant bastard. Even if he hadn't killed anyone, the guy deserved to be locked up. She remembered the look he'd given her when she was out on the dock and shivered. Al was right about watching her back—she'd feel safer if Steve Drake were still in jail. Hopefully, Sanders would nail them to the wall, and they'd be sent away for a very long time.

Mickey was still determined to find out who was responsible for George's death. If he was killed on the dock that night, how could it have happened without Tim seeing anything? And there was Chen's driver to think about. Maybe he had seen something that would help her fill in the blanks.

Troubled Waters

Mickey opened the door to the room and yelled for Colin. Hearing no reply, she debated whether to wait for him and decided to leave him a note. Looking around for a good place to put it, her eyes settled on the refrigerator. That would be perfect. She clamped the note in the door and grabbed her backpack on the way out.

CHAPTER *Twenty-Four*

*B*rad Sanders moved Bart to an unoccupied office for questioning and gave him some coffee and donuts. While Bart inhaled several sugar-coated donuts and gulped the coffee, Sanders sat across the table making notes. He gave Bart time to finish before starting in with his questions.

"So, tell me Bart, how long have you worked for the Drake brothers?"

"Since last summer. They were down in the sound, working a geo-duck tract, and needed a tender."

"Do they pay you good?" Sanders asked.

"It's alright, I guess. Urchins pay a hell of a lot better than diving for ducks, and I live on the boat, so it's not like I got any big expenses. It sure beats workin' at McDonald's, if that's what you mean," Bart said, sounding a little defensive.

Sanders nodded and leaned back in his chair. "So, were you on board when they brought *Intruder* out to Neah Bay?"

"Yeah, Ted and I made the run together. I think it must've been that Wednesday before the season started. Steve cruised out in his fancy little car 'cause he doesn't trust anyone else to drive it," Bart added, scowling.

Sanders chewed on a wooden toothpick in the corner of his mouth while he took notes. "Tell me about harvesting the urchins. How many days did you work before the season opened?"

Bart squirmed under Sander's gaze. "We went out on Thursday to do some surveying, and I thought that's all we were gonna do. But the next day, they started bagging urchins and leaving 'em on the bottom with a little float to mark the spot. What was I supposed to do? I tried telling 'em it was a bad idea. I told 'em we'd be in deep shit if somebody found out."

"And what was their response to that?" Sanders asked him.

"Steve gave me one of his mean looks and asked how anyone was gonna know. Then he threatened me and said if I ever told anyone, he'd make sure they never found my body." Bart shifted nervously in his seat and fell silent, a troubled look on his face.

Sanders looked up from his notes and spoke in a reassuring voice. "The Drake brothers are not going to walk on this one. We have a solid case, and with their past records, they'll end up doing hard time. They won't be a threat to anyone once we get them behind bars."

Bart didn't look entirely convinced. "Will I have to show up in court and testify?"

"That shouldn't be necessary. We'll take a deposition of your testimony and submit it to the judge, along with the rest of the evidence," Sanders said.

"Well, that sounds okay, I guess. But, what's gonna happen to me? What do I get outta this deal?"

"This is the deal, Bart. If you give us your full cooperation, the prosecutor will drop your charge to a misdemeanor and you'll be released without bail. I can't make any guarantees on how the judge will handle it, but you'll probably get off with a fine and suspended sentence."

Bart nodded, and the worried look slowly faded.

Sanders prompted him with a question. "So, how many days did it take to harvest the urchins?"

"We worked two days with both of 'em in the water, and the place must've been loaded, 'cause they were doing thirty minute bags. The second day—just before dark—we brought the bags on board, then sat on the hook 'til around midnight, waiting to come in."

"Where did you unload?"

"At the old fuel dock. A young Indian dude was running the hoist."
Bart paused as the door squeaked open behind him, and a Makah
policeman poked his head in.

Sanders looked up in irritation. "Didn't I say no interruptions?"

"Sorry, but you have an urgent phone call, and the Chief thinks you
better take it. I can stay 'til you get back."

Sanders nodded and left the room, wondering what the hell was so
urgent that it couldn't wait thirty minutes.

*   *   *   *   *

Holt fumed while he waited for Sanders to come on the line,
annoyed that he hadn't been told that poachers were unloading their
boat the night George was killed. If he'd known that, he might be
pursuing something worthwhile, instead of wasting his time on a
wild goose chase.

After leaving Sheri's place, Holt had used his cell phone to check in
with the office and learned that Carl had called to say he wanted to
come in and make a statement. It looked like his hot lead was turning
into a dead end. But, he still had to follow through, question Carl and
check out his alibi. Holt ground his teeth together in frustration. This
investigation was spinning out of control, and he didn't like it one bit.

"Officer Sanders here," a voice announced curtly.

"Officer Sanders, this is James Holt, Deputy Coroner of Clallam
County. I'm investigating a homicide, and I understand that you have
turned up evidence which may be crucial to my case. I don't know what
you think you're doing withholding important evidence, but I won't
tolerate any interference."

"Now, wait just a minute. It would help if I knew what…"

"Don't play games with me, Sanders. You know exactly what I'm talking about. And I don't give a shit about you making a lousy poaching

bust when I got a murder case on my hands. Those glasses should have been turned over to the police immediately."

"Listen, I don't know what the hell you're talking about. And if you don't want me hanging up in the next two seconds, you'd better start at the beginning. Who was murdered, dammit?"

Holt drew in a deep breath and struggled to control his anger. "I'm talking about the murder of George Kessler. Mickey Sutter called Mrs. Kessler half an hour ago and told her that his death may be linked to a poaching operation that you're investigating."

"What?" Sanders said, stunned by the news. "I thought Kessler's death was an accident."

"The autopsy proved otherwise," Holt answered in a tired voice.

"Well, if your department wants my cooperation, it would certainly help if they'd share information once in awhile," he remarked acidly. "But you still haven't explained how this ties in with the poaching incident."

Holt rubbed his forehead and exhaled loudly. "The poachers were offloading urchins the night Kessler arrived, and Ms. Sutter, who is playing private detective, seems to think Kessler might have caught them in the act. Apparently, some diver found a pair of glasses in the water next to the dock where they unloaded, and she thinks they belong to Kessler. And you're telling me you don't know any of this?" Holt added impatiently.

"Ten minutes ago, I didn't even know Kessler had been murdered," Sanders reminded him. "I haven't talked to Mickey for a couple of days, but it sounds like she may be onto something. And I have to say, I do trust her intuition. She was the one who found out about the poaching in the first place, and none of it would have come together without her help." Sanders was still puzzled about one thing. "What made you think I have these mystery glasses?"

"When Mickey was on the phone with Sheri Kessler, she said that you were investigating the poaching violation, and I assumed she would turn the glasses over to you. I guess maybe I jumped to the wrong conclusion," Holt admitted grudgingly. If Sanders expected an apology, that was all he was going to get. "Uh, by the way, when Kessler was found, he had one of your business cards in his shirt pocket. It didn't seem important at first, but now that I've learned about the poaching, it takes on a whole new meaning."

Sanders was quiet, trying to absorb this new information. He had a strong case against the Drake brothers, especially with Bart's testimony, but murder would change everything.

After a short silence, Holt continued. "I really need to locate those glasses, but I'm going to be tied up in Anacortes for at least another hour. I'd sure appreciate it if you could handle that for me, since you're already out there."

Sanders glanced at his watch. "Yes, I can do that just as soon as I finish up with a witness in the poaching case. After hearing Mickey's theory, I definitely have some new questions for him, and maybe he'll shed some light on the Kessler connection."

Holt was frustrated that he wasn't there to do the questioning himself, but it couldn't be helped. After asking Sanders where he could be reached later on, Holt hung up the phone. In fifteen minutes, he was due to meet Carl at the local police station. Letting out a sigh, he started the engine and pulled away from the curb.

CHAPTER *Twenty-Five*

*F*or most people, the drive from Neah Bay to Port Angeles took an hour and forty-five minutes, but not Mickey. She liked to speed, and it rarely took her more than an hour and a half. Today, she was in a bigger hurry than usual because she wanted to drop the glasses off with Holt and talk to Chen about the poaching. Pushing her speed up to fifty, she took the next series of curves without touching the brakes, her mind on George.

Rounding a corner, she was suddenly brought back to the present by a flagger waving his sign. She braked hard, stopping just short of a logging truck, then groaned loudly as she saw that the road ahead was blocked by a huge mudslide. The bluff above the highway had been clearcut a few years ago, and the road had been plagued by slides ever since. Mickey turned off the engine and cursed her bad luck. It was going to take awhile to clear this mess. She watched as a front loader picked up a scoop of mud and dumped it over the bank into the water, adding more silt to the brown current that swept along the shoreline. She sighed and leaned her head back against the seat. Nothing to do, but wait.

*   *   *   *   *

As soon as Brad Sanders stepped into the room, Bart asked him, "When do I get outta here? You said if I cooperated, you'd turn me loose."

Sanders didn't answer immediately, his piercing gaze fixed on Bart while he settled into a chair and tucked a wad of snuff inside his lip. When he finally spoke, there was a hard edge to his voice.

"Tell you what, Bart, I've got a problem. I don't think you've been entirely honest with me."

"What the hell do you mean?" Bart said, his face twisting into a scowl.

Sanders slammed his hands down on the table and leaned forward, his words coming out in a growl, "You haven't said one word about the guy who caught you unloading the urchins."

"Man, what're you talking about? Nobody caught us!" Bart protested, looking confused.

"Don't play stupid with me, or all deals are off. You want to be a partner in murder, then plan on going away for a very long time. Or start over, and tell me the whole story this time." Sanders eased back down in his seat and waited for Bart to respond.

Bart looked at him in disbelief, shaking his head from side to side. "You're crazy, man. There's nothin' to tell. Where you comin' up with this murder shit? I been straight with you and now you wanna say, no deal? Bullshit! I want a lawyer."

Sanders spit into an empty cup and stared at Bart with a tight expression. "A man was murdered at the fuel dock Saturday night–the same night you were offloading urchins. I want to know everything that happened that night—everything you saw, everything you heard, and I want the name of everyone who was there and what they were doing— every single detail. And Bart, if I find out you're lying to me....you will regret it. I guarantee."

"I been tellin' you the truth, man. I don't know nothin' about anyone gettin' killed." Bart brushed the hair out of his face and gave Sanders a questioning look. "Hey, you talkin' about the guy they found dead on his boat? I heard that was an accident, man!"

Sanders picked some lint off the knee of his trousers and considered what to say next. "Someone wanted it to look like an accident, but it was murder. That's a whole new ball game. I don't know how the D.A. will handle it, but I can tell you this—if you cooperate, it will go down better for you. If you're straight with me, I'll talk to the D.A. and see what I can do."

"How do I know I can trust you?"

"You'll have to make up your own mind on that," Sanders said, holding Bart's gaze until he looked away.

Bart stared off into space for several seconds, then looked back at Sanders. "What do you wanna know?"

*   *   *   *   *

Inside the motel room, Colin kicked his shoes off and padded into the kitchen, his wet socks leaving a trail of sand from the beach. Stripping off his rain-soaked sweatshirt, he hung it over the back of a chair, then grabbed a glass from the dish rack and filled it with cold tap water. After downing his second glassful, he spotted the note hanging from the door of the refrigerator and smiled. Mickey had him figured out.

Colin removed the note, grabbing an apple while he had the door open, and sat down to read.

"Hi Colin—Gone to P.A. for groceries and BEER! Picked up the glasses from Al and I'm sure they're George's. Couldn't get through to Sanders or Holt, but plan to stop by Sheriff's office on way home. Hope Holt is back–I've got a few things to say to him! I'm betting Steve Drake is guilty as sin, but I need proof! Been wondering who Chen's driver was. Maybe he saw something. I'm going to stop by Chen's plant to see if I can weasel some information out of him. Wish me luck! Love, Mickey

P.S. Drake brothers are already out on bail! Aarrgghh!"

Colin sat upright, frowning at the note. Maybe he was just being overprotective, but he felt uneasy all of a sudden and wished he'd gone with her. Mickey had a knack for stirring up trouble, and he wished he was there to keep an eye on her.

Chapter *Twenty-Six*

*B*rad Sanders felt stymied. After listening to Bart's story for the third time, he was no closer to finding out what happened to George Kessler than he had been an hour ago, so he tried another tack.

"Bart, think back to the unloading for a minute. Did you hear anything unusual while you were working? Any kind of a loud noise? Sound of another boat, people yelling, something like that."

"That hoist makes such a racket, I couldn't hear nothin'. It made me nervous. Figured if we were gonna get busted, that's when it would happen. I just wanted to get those bags off the boat and be done with it." He stopped, frowning as he tried to remember. "But, there was somethin'. I was hooking up some bags, so the winch was quiet, and I thought I might've heard a boat. Didn't hear nothin' after that and thought I was just being paranoid."

Sander's pulse picked up, and he leaned forward, his arms resting on the table. "Did anyone leave the unloading area after that? I want you to take your time and think about it." Sanders clenched the pencil so tightly the tips of his fingers were turning white, and he forced his hand to relax.

Bart shook his head. "No, man, I don't think so. It's like I been telling you all along. The Indian kid was runnin' the hoist, and Steve was up there reading the scale, along with the truck driver. They didn't trust each other to keep the weight, so they were right there the whole time, an' Ted was on the boat with me."

"What about after you finished unloading? What happened then?"

"Soon as we got all the bags off, the driver was pacing back an' forth on the dock while the Indian kid loaded the totes in his truck, and he was outta' there. Then, Steve came back down on the boat, used a calculator to add up the weight and said he was gonna go find Chen and collect our money."

Sanders broke the tip of his pencil against the paper and nearly shouted his response. "Chen was there? Why didn't you tell me before?"

Bart jumped in his chair, startled by the sudden intensity. "I didn't think of it 'til now. I never saw him, but he musta' been there. Steve wasn't gone five minutes an' he came back with a wad of hundred dollar bills. Paid me twelve-hundred bucks. Best payday I ever had." His face fell as he thought about the money. "Ahhh, man. What's gonna happen to the money I had stashed on the boat?"

Sanders, deep in concentration, ignored the question. He was shocked to learn that Chen had been there, but it was beginning to make sense now. If Chen had kept a low profile, that would explain why Tim hadn't seen him, and it also meant that he was off by himself during the unloading.

Sanders thought back to his phone conversation with Chen. When he questioned him about the totes, Chen had sounded extremely nervous, and when he confronted him about the fresh urchin spines on the dock, Chen sounded close to panic. Sanders had written it off as a reaction to the threat of felony poaching charges. But why didn't Chen make a deal when given the chance? Did he expect Drake to cover for him? That would be like trusting a bank robber to make your deposits. Maybe the real reason for his panic was that Chen had something more to hide.

The glasses were the key. If they belonged to Kessler, and he could be placed at the dock that night, it was time to take a serious look at everyone who'd been there. With a new sense of urgency, Sanders opened the door and called for a deputy. Christ, he hoped Mickey hadn't left town for the closure.

"You can take him back to his cell now," Sanders said, gathering his notes.

"Back to a cell?" Bart protested. "Hey, when do I get released? You said…"

Sanders glanced at Bart. "A Sheriff's deputy will be here shortly to take you to Port Angeles. I'll talk with the D.A. as soon as I have a chance, but you'll just have to be patient."

Ignoring Bart's strident objections, he hurried down the hall.

*   *   *   *   *

Startled by a loud knock at the door, Colin set down the remains of his sandwich and went to see who was there. Mickey wasn't due back for a few hours yet, and most of the divers had left town, so Colin had no idea who it could be. But, the last person he expected to see was Brad Sanders.

"Is Mickey here?" Sanders asked with barely concealed impatience, his eyes scanning the room behind Colin as he spoke.

"No. She went to Port Angeles to run some errands, and I'm not sure when she'll be back." Colin caught the flash of disappointment and wondered what was up. Sanders wasn't the type to drop by for a social visit, and he seemed unusually tense, so Colin invited him in and asked what was happening.

"There's something I wanted to ask her about, but maybe you can tell me. Did she happen to mention anything about a pair of glasses some-one found by the old fuel dock?"

Colin felt his insides tighten up a notch. "Yeah…it came up last night at dinner. Rick Kautzman found the glasses when he went after his fuel cap, and he left 'em with Al. Mickey got the idea that they might have belonged to George, so she picked them up from Al this morning and took 'em to P.A. with her. She plans to turn them in at the Sheriff's office."

"Glad to hear it," Sanders said, looking greatly relieved. "When did she leave, by the way?"

"Not exactly sure, but it was probably about forty-five minutes ago. I was out running, and she left me a note." Colin picked it up and handed it to Sanders. "Actually, I've been kind of worried since she left. Mickey has convinced herself that Steve Drake murdered George, and she's determined to prove it."

Sanders frowned as he read the note and cursed under his breath. "I'd better get going," he said abruptly. Handing the note back, he started for the door, but Colin moved to block his path.

"Wait a minute! Something in her note set you off, and I want to know what it is."

Sanders hesitated before speaking. "It involves a murder investigation, and I'm not free to discuss the details."

"I don't care about the damn details. I just want to know if Mickey's in danger." They glared at each other for several seconds, keenly aware of the unspoken message passing between them.

"Can you keep your mouth shut?" Sanders said finally.

"Damn straight."

"I think she may be getting herself into a pile of trouble. Chen has denied any knowledge of the poaching—-even when he was offered a deal–and I just learned that he was here in town the night they offloaded the urchins." Sanders exhaled loudly before continuing. "As far as I know, he's the only person who is unaccounted for. If he killed Kessler, and Mickey pressures him for information—there's no telling how he'll react."

"Son-of-a bitch!" Colin exclaimed.

"I'd better get going. If Mickey does her shopping before going to see Chen, I can probably beat her there. I'll call you later and let you know what's happening."

"Screw that! I'm coming with you," Colin said, grabbing his shoes. Sanders didn't stop to argue—he was already on his way out the door.

CHAPTER *Twenty-Seven*

Scott Chen thumbed through a stack of overdue bills on his desk, punching in the numbers on a calculator. The total amount was staggering, but he had no intention of paying it anyway. It was just an amusing way to pass the time while he waited for the workers to finish up and go home. The unpaid bills would be his bonus, a going-away gift from people he'd done business with.

As the door to his office opened, Chen looked up to see the young crew boss standing hesitantly in the doorway. Peter Sun nodded politely, his black hair flopping forward on his head. Long on top and short on the sides, it looked like someone had put a bowl on his head and shaved everything below. Chen thought he looked silly. Peter stepped into the office, but waited for a nod from Chen before rattling off his report in Korean.

"The crew has finished and the trays are in the cooler. It was a small load today, but the quality looks very good. They are cleaning up now."

"Excellent. You handled things quite well today, Mr. Sun. Maybe soon you will be ready to take over as plant manager."

Sun beamed with pleasure at the compliment, and Chen smiled to mask his deceit. The young fool knew nothing about running a processing plant, but Chen had needed someone to fill in after sending Mr. Kashimoto, his full-time manager, back to Oregon. The man was too sharp, and Chen wanted Kashimoto out of the way while he made his arrangements. He'd used the excuse that they needed him at the other plant, telling him the weather forecast was favorable and they expected lots of product.

"Thank you, that will be all," Chen said, dismissing him.

Sun's smile faded, and he fidgeted nervously in front of the desk. "Uh, Mr. Chen…there was something I wanted to ask you. We were wondering…"

"Speak your mind, Mr. Sun. I do not have all day."

"Yes sir. The crew would like to know…uh, they were all wondering if we would be paid today."

The smile remained plastered on Chen's face, and he spoke carefully, his voice conveying just the right balance of regret and reassurance.

"Please, let me explain. A most unfortunate incident at the bank caused a very large deposit to be credited to the wrong account. I have been on the phone for over an hour, and the bank manager assures me that the money will be transferred to my account today."

Chen rubbed his chin and sighed heavily. "It has been a disaster. Angry divers are calling me, saying my checks are no good, and when I try to explain, they do not listen. I do not want this kind of problem with my valuable workers. Before issuing your checks, I would like to make sure the money has been credited to my account." Chen smiled in apology. "Please ask the crew to wait just one more day."

Peter looked unhappy, but he nodded and turned to go.

"Please tell them that I will write checks first thing tomorrow morning and add ten-percent bonus to everyone's pay—a small reward for their loyalty."

A broad smile spread across Sun's face, and he left in a hurry, closing the door on his way out. Chen silently congratulated himself for the skillful move. The promise of a bonus would appease his workers, and they would leave without giving him trouble. Tomorrow, when they returned to pick up their checks, they would find everything locked up and a note on the door saying he'd been called away to deal with an emergency. By the time they figured out the truth, it would be too late.

Troubled Waters

Glancing at the clock, Chen saw it was nearly two. Time was growing short, and there was still much to be done. Reaching into the side drawer of his desk, he pulled out the yellow pages for the Seattle area and scanned motel listings, jotting down the ones near Sea-Tac airport. Just as he was reaching for the phone, it began to ring.

Hand poised in midair, Chen hesitated, trying to decide whether to answer or not. It was probably another diver, calling to complain about his money. He'd lost count of the number of calls, but it seemed like he'd heard from every diver in the fleet. Most of them calmed down quickly when he explained the situation, but he was tired of talking to these scum. On the other hand, he did not want some angry diver showing up on his doorstep. Better to handle it over the phone, Chen thought and forced himself to answer cheerfully.

"Good afternoon, Chen Trading Company."

"Scott Chen, what is going on?" His wife's shrill voice rang in his ear. "You said you would call me right back, and I have heard nothing from you since yesterday."

"I am very sorry, dear. It has been a most hectic day. I was just reaching for the phone to call you. Please accept my apologies."

She gave a snort of disbelief, then fell silent. When she spoke again, her tone was softer. "When are you coming home?"

"Ahhh…something has come up. A little problem I must take care of before I leave. It may be a couple of days before I can…"

"What problem? I do not understand. You promised…"

"I know, dear, and I am very sorry. I will try to take care of things very quickly."

"What are you talking about? You speak in riddles. Did you pay the bills? You never tell me what is going on anymore."

"I told you I would take care of it, dear. Please, do not worry yourself over these things." Chen's mind raced frantically. He wasn't planning on coming home, ever again, but if she reported him missing right away, it could ruin everything. He should have been ready with an excuse,

- 176 -

something that would not arouse her suspicion. "Everything is fine—just a few minor problems with the plant."

The line was silent for several seconds, and Chen's stomach fluttered anxiously.

"Damn you, Scott Chen. Tell me the truth. Are you seeing another woman?" she demanded.

The accusation caught Chen by surprise, but he realized that it gave him the perfect excuse. "It has been a trying week, and I need some time to myself," he stated calmly, then added, "When we married, I only promised that I would be discreet."

"You can take your lousy promise and go to hell," she screamed, slamming the phone down.

Chen jumped at the crashing sound, but he was smiling as he cradled the receiver. This was working out perfectly. Tonight, after delivering the last shipment of roe to the airport, he would stay at the Airport Hilton. He called to reserve a suite in the name of Charles Scott, then decided a celebration was in order. And what better way to celebrate than in the company of a beautiful woman. This time he would not leave things to chance. Chen searched his wallet for a tattered business card and dialed the number on the back.

"Eve's Escort Service. How may we help you?" the woman inquired in a rich, silky voice.

Chen requested a companion for the evening, then waited on hold while she checked his references. After querying him about his tastes, she gave him a name.

"Iris, wearing the flower she is named after, will be waiting for you in the lounge of the Airport Hilton at eight o'clock this evening." Chen hung up and leaned back in his chair, enjoying the tingling sense of anticipation.

*　　*　　*　　*　　*

Sanders forced himself to slow down while passing through the small community of Clallam Bay, then put his foot in it when he hit the straightaway leaving town. The Blazer rumbled along like a tank as the speedometer reached eighty-five, and Colin, who had been silent since leaving Neah Bay, watched the rain-soaked fields and mossy trees on the banks of the river rush by in a blur.

Reaching the turnoff for Highway 112, Sanders decided that the less traveled road along the river would be his best bet. The alternate route which passed by Lake Crescent had more straight stretches, but was also likely to have more traffic. Slowing to forty, he cut the corner and felt the tires skid slightly on the wet pavement. The twisty, curvy road followed the path of the river through a forest of towering hemlocks, and some of the massive trees were barely off the pavement.

Sanders didn't slow down as he reached the next set of curves, just shaved the corners on both sides of the road, maintaining an almost straight path. Colin clutched the armrest with a white-knuckled grip, his face set in a mask of indifference. He'd ridden with some crazy bastard Marines before, but this guy was totally nuts. As a giant tree flashed past Colin's window, he knew they were too close. The scarred trunk caught the outside edge of the mirror, slamming it back against the door panel like a shot.

"Holy shit!" Colin shouted.

Sanders looked over and grinned. He loved the excitement of a chase, the rush of adrenaline in his veins making him feel alive. "We having fun yet?"

"Oh, yeah! I only wish I was wearing my wetsuit. Then maybe I wouldn't freeze my balls off when we end up in the river."

"Hey, there's an idea. Snag a steelhead while you're swimming around. Of course, I'd have to cite you for not using a barb-less hook," Sanders said, laughing at his own joke. He was enjoying himself.

Colin rolled his eyes and shook his head, but a faint smile crept onto his face. The road soon parted company with the river, leaving the forest behind, and straightened out in a steep downgrade over-looking the straits. Colin breathed a sigh of relief and shifted in his seat to look at Sanders.

"Tell me something. Do you think that little weasel, Chen, killed George?"

Sanders' expression turned serious, all humor gone from his eyes.

"Let me put it this way—the guy is shifty. He lied about the poaching and wouldn't even talk about making a deal. I still don't understand why he didn't jump at my offer–unless he's got something more to hide than buying illegal urchins."

Sanders picked up his radio mike and tried reaching the dispatcher in Port Angeles. After a couple of tries, he gave up. "We must be in a dead zone," he said, then explained that he was going to request a Sheriff's Deputy be sent over to Chen's plant, just to be on the safe side. Sanders frowned, wishing he'd thought of it earlier. Tucked up against these hills, they might be out of radio contact until they were damn near in Port Angeles themselves.

"I wish Mickey hadn't charged off by herself on this one," Sanders told Colin. "I've got a bad feeling about this guy."

Colin's face became grim, and he tightened his seatbelt. "Can you make this heap go any faster?"

Sanders raised one eyebrow in a questioning look.

"Just keep us on the road, and I won't say a word," Colin told him.

"O-kaaay," Sanders said, allowing himself a wicked grin as he pushed the pedal to the floor.

CHAPTER *Twenty-Eight*

_W_ hile the checker rang up her groceries, Mickey scanned the headlines on the tabloids and shook her head in amazement. Baby born with two heads, latest Elvis sighting confirmed, how to lose twenty pounds without going on a diet. Good grief! The scary part was, she suspected some people actually believed that crap.

"Would you prefer paper or plastic?" the young woman asked, already reaching for the plastic.

"Paper," Mickey replied, feeling around in her backpack for the checkbook. "And I'd like them double bagged, please."

The woman looked irritated at the request, and she made a big production out of putting the bags together. Her long, dark hair was tied back in a pony tail, emphasizing her thin face and pasty white skin, and Mickey couldn't help noticing her frail, skinny arms as she placed the bags in the cart.

"Do you need some help out with this, ma'am?" she said, her tone suggesting that she'd be doing Mickey a big favor.

"Don't put yourself out, sweetie, I think I can handle it." Mickey was tempted to reach over and gently squeeze the woman's arm as though checking for muscle, but she restrained herself and reached for the cart instead.

Outside the store, Mickey stopped at the phone booth and fished out the business card Holt had given her. After four rings, the dispatcher answered and informed Mickey that Holt was out of the office.

D.J. Ferguson

"Can you tell me when he'll be back?" Mickey pushed the cart closer to the building, trying to shelter it from the rain.

"He's expected back sometime this afternoon. Would you like to leave a message?"

"No thanks, I'll call back later." Mickey hung up and stared out across the parking lot. Now what? She'd planned on seeing Holt before stopping by Chen's plant on her way out of town, but that wasn't going to work. Oh, well. If she had to come back into town to give Holt a piece of her mind, it was worth it.

She briefly considered calling ahead to make sure Chen was there, but decided against it. He wouldn't be eager to talk with her—not after she'd ruined their little price-fixing scheme. It would probably be better to just show up.

*   *   *   *   *

Chen had shed his coat and tie, draping them over the back of a chair, and now sat at his desk, impatiently drumming his fingers on the keys of his laptop computer. An atlas was propped open to the Bahamas, the city of Nassau circled in red, and while waiting for the next screen to materialize, Chen gazed at the map, his mind conjuring up images of lush green islands with sandy white beaches and towering palm trees, surrounded by crystal clear water. He wished he were already there, but at this rate, he'd die of old age first.

He'd been on-line for twenty minutes now, trying to obtain flight information and reserve himself a seat, and he had accomplished absolutely nothing. Disgusted, Chen hit the escape button until he was back at the original menu and started over. Hitting the keys harder than necessary, he typed in the request for airlines, flight information, international, then city. After a couple of minutes, it gave him a list of airlines serving the Bahamas, and he breathed a sigh of relief.

Spotting a familiar name, Chen clicked on Continental, but nothing happened. He then tried typing in their website address, and after waiting what seemed an eternity, a message appeared on the screen: "Unable to respond, server may be busy."

"Dammit all to hell!" Chen shouted and switched off the computer. Unplugging the phone line from the modem, he nearly yanked the end off the cord, but managed to get it plugged back into the phone and dialed the toll free number for the airline. A woman's voice answered cheerfully, and Chen snapped at her, complaining about Continental's on-line service.

"I'm sorry you had trouble, sir. How may I assist you?"

Checking his temper, he asked about flights from Sea-Tac to Nassau.

"We have flights twice weekly, leaving on Sundays and Thursdays, with a connection in Houston. What day do you wish to travel, sir?"

Chen swivelled his chair to look at the calendar. Today was Thursday, so it would have to be Sunday. "December 7th," he replied.

"Regular fare is five hundred and twenty-three dollars, plus tax. May I have your name, please?"

Chen started to give his real name, but caught himself. "My name is Scott, Charles Scott, and I wish to fly first class."

"No problem, sir. That will be flight number four-twenty-three, leaving Seattle at six-thirty a.m. on Sunday, December 7," she replied. "The round trip fare for first-class is sixteen-hundred and fifty-five dollars, plus tax. How do you wish to pay for this?"

Chen winced at the price, then reminded himself that he could afford it now. He started to reach for his company credit card, then stopped himself and cursed under his breath. What was he thinking? A stupid move like that would leave a paper trail even a blind person could follow.

"I would like to have a window seat," he said, stalling for time.

"Yes, sir. I will put in your request, but I can't promise you one will be available."

"Very well. I will pick up my ticket at the airport on the morning of my flight and pay for it then."

Hanging up the phone, he chided himself for being so unprepared. He needed a plan. Tomorrow, first thing, he would go to the bank and empty the personal checking account. That would give him plenty of cash to pay for the plane ticket and leave him with some traveling money. By the time his wife found out that her checks were bouncing, he'd be long gone. When the rest of the funds arrived from Japan, he would withdraw the entire balance in the form of a cashier's check. Easy to carry on the plane, and no questions asked when he opened a new account in Nassau. It was coming together nicely.

Chen was startled by the sound of footsteps on the stairs and wondered who it could be. His workers had left some time ago, and Peter Sun was supposed to have locked up on his way out. Moving quickly, Chen grabbed all his notes and hid them under the atlas, then started for the door just as it began to open.

CHAPTER *Twenty-Nine*

"What are you doing here?" Chen asked, not bothering to say hello. "You have no business here."

"Nice to see you, too," Mickey said, smiling at his discomfort. "I just stopped by to ask you about something. Mind if I sit down?" She sat without waiting for a reply and watched Chen's face as he struggled to hide his irritation.

"I am very busy, and I do not see why I should make time for someone who does not even sell me their urchins," Chen said, seating himself behind the desk.

"I would gladly sell to you, if you offered a decent price," Mickey responded, then kicked herself for saying it. Starting an argument was not a good way to gain his cooperation, but it would take an awful lot of restraint on her part to be polite.

"Decent price?" he scoffed. "I pay fair price all the time, but you divers are never satisfied. You always demand more."

"You're absolutely right, Chen. Greed is my middle name. But that's not why I'm here." Mickey decided she might as well be blunt. "I'm here to find out who was driving the truck when you bought that load of illegal urchins from the Drake brothers."

"I know nothing about any poaching," Chen said indignantly.

"Oh, cut the crap, Chen. The Drake brothers have been selling to you forever, and they wouldn't go to another buyer with an illegal load. They'd want to deal with someone they know, and you're shifty enough to do it. Besides, the urchins went into your totes."

"I already talked to Fisheries about this. Someone else must have used my totes."

"Yeah, right. You can deny it until you're blue in the face, but we both know you're lying." She leaned her elbows on the edge of Chen's desk and watched his face turn flush with rage.

"I will not listen to your silly accusations. You must leave now," he said, his voice rising in pitch. It was bad enough that she came into his office uninvited, but then she–a mere woman—had the gall to challenge him. Unbelievable!

"Save the act for somebody else, Chen. You're not getting rid of me that easily. I'm not here to play games. The night those urchins were unloaded, a good friend of mine was murdered. I think George caught them in the act, and one of those creeps killed him. And I intend to find out who did it." Mickey glared at him, matching his anger with her own.

"What? How could…that is crazy…" Chen stammered. He was so shocked at the mention of murder, he barely heard the rest of what she was saying. News of Kessler's death had spread like wildfire, and there had been no hint that anyone suspected foul play. It was just what Chen had hoped for. But now this! He felt a sudden, stabbing pain in his temple.

"Listen, Chen, no one's going to give a rip about poaching when they have a murder case on their hands. If you help bust the person who killed George, I doubt they'd even charge you for buying illegal urchins. And you don't owe Steve Drake any loyalty. If it were the other way around—he'd drop the dime on you in a second. Just tell me the name of your truck driver. Maybe he saw something that night."

Chen struggled to concentrate on what she was saying, and it slowly dawned on him that Mickey suspected Steve Drake of killing her friend. He felt a surge of relief, but it was short-lived. Both Drake and his driver knew he'd been there that night, and it wouldn't take the police long to find out he'd been off by himself while everyone else was busy unloading the urchins. Christ, he'd be their number one suspect. Jumbled thoughts raced through his mind, and Chen fought to control the rising feeling of panic.

"This is terrible shock to me....everyone say it was an accident. I do not understand why you think he was murdered."

"I spoke with Sheri Kessler this morning, and she told me they did an autopsy. The police are convinced it was no accident."

"But....I still do not see. Just because it happened same night as poaching does not mean it had anything to do with urchins." Slowly recovering his composure, Chen smoothed back his hair and forced himself to meet Mickey's gaze. Just a couple more days was all he needed, and none of this would matter.

"I talked with George on the radio that evening, and he said he expected to arrive in Neah Bay sometime after midnight. We know they started offloading urchins at about half past twelve, so George could easily have stumbled onto their operation. I don't know exactly what happened, but my guess is he confronted them." Mickey took in a deep breath and let it out slowly.

When she spoke again, her voice was low and intense. "Colin and I found George's body the next morning. Someone wanted it to look like an accident, but they didn't quite pull it off. I can't prove it yet, but I'm dead sure somebody on that dock killed him."

Chen smiled apologetically and shook his head. "Please accept my sympathies, but I cannot help you. I did not buy any illegal urchins. Maybe if you try talking to other processors, they can help you." He didn't give a damn whether she believed him or not. That was his story and he was sticking to it. Chen stood up and disconnected the power cord to the laptop, then reached for the soft leather carrying case.

Silently, she watched him slide the computer into its case, zip it shut, and check his watch as though late for an appointment. Ignoring the hint, Mickey remained seated.

"I promised my wife to be home for dinner, and I have very long drive," Chen said, gesturing toward the door. "You must go now."

D.J. Ferguson

"You lying bastard," she said, her eyes flashing with anger. "You bought those urchins. You hired that driver. And I'm not leaving until I get his name."

"This is ridiculous." Chen fought the urge to grab Mickey and shove her out the door. God, he hated her! But he mustn't let the trouble-making bitch provoke him. "You waste my time with these fantastic stories, but you have no proof. Sit here all night if you wish. I am leaving."

"You're wrong about that, Chen. I do have proof, and I'm on my way right now to see the man in charge of the investigation. I'll be sure and tell him how cooperative you've been." Mickey jumped to her feet and took a couple of steps toward the door.

"What do you mean?" Chen asked, feeling a quiver of alarm.

"I have evidence that proves George was at the dock where they unloaded."

"How is that possible? Maybe you dream up this whole story, so you can play private eye."

Mickey gave him a scorching look. "George's glasses were found underwater right next to the pier where they unloaded. Hardly a dream, and I'm sure the police won't think so."

The color drained from Chen's face, and he sank down into his chair. His head was throbbing, making it hard to concentrate. He'd quit worrying about the poaching days ago, knowing he'd be long gone before anything could happen. Even if they filed charges, it would be weeks before he had to appear in court, and they wouldn't start looking for him until he failed to show up. But murder, that was altogether different. Once the police discovered he'd been on the dock that night, they would hound him with questions and watch his every move.

Chen noticed Mickey looking at him curiously and tried to cover himself by saying, "This comes as a great shock to me. I just cannot believe someone would do such a thing. These glasses—are you sure they are his?"

Frown lines creased Mickey's forehead. "George wore his glasses all the time, but they weren't there when we found his body. It didn't register at the time, but when someone mentioned finding glasses by the fuel dock, I got to thinking and called Sheri. She told me that his glasses weren't returned with his other belongings. This pair looks familiar, and I'm betting they're his. It will be easy enough for the police to prove, once they get them."

Chen was only half listening. The bitch had ruined what should have been a profitable season, and now here she was stirring up even more trouble. It took a couple of seconds for her last words to sink in.

"What? The police do not have these glasses yet?"

"No, they're still in my truck. I'm going to drop them off before I leave town. The coroner was out of his office, so I came here first—hoping you'd listen to reason. That turned out to be a big waste of time," she added sarcastically.

"Wait...please...I need a minute to think. I do not wish to get in trouble, but if murder is involved–this is very serious matter. It changes everything." Chen hoped he sounded sincere. If he could get the glasses and destroy them, then he'd be in the clear. Somehow, he must stop her from leaving and find a way to catch her off guard.

"Maybe you are right. I think I should go to the police and make a statement."

Mickey eyed him suspiciously, surprised at the sudden change of heart. "That would be the smart thing to do. The way our court system works, you'll get the best possible deal if you go to them and volunteer the information."

"I will do it, then. We can go together, yes? I just need to lock up, and I can follow you in my car."

Mickey wasn't sure what caused him to change his mind, but she was pleased that he intended to cooperate. "That's a great idea. You're doing the right thing."

D.J. Ferguson

Trembling with nervousness, Chen glanced around the room as though checking to make sure he had everything, then lifted his jacket from the chair and patted his pocket for the keys. Picking up the computer case, he nodded that he was ready.

"After you," he said politely, holding the door.

CHAPTER *Thirty*

*A*s Sanders made a fast turn into the gravel parking lot, Colin leaned forward and spotted Mickey's blue pickup parked in front of the processing plant. "There's her truck, but I don't see any Sheriff's car."

Brad Sanders frowned. He'd called in almost fifteen minutes ago, asking them to send some deputies out to check on things. So, where the hell were they? The only other vehicles in sight were a truck backed up to a loading bay at the corner of the building and a black Lincoln Continental, which Sanders took to be Chen's. Sanders steered toward the far end of the lot, jerking to a stop just inches away from the car's back bumper. If Chen got any ideas about making a fast getaway, he was in for a rude surprise.

Colin already had his seatbelt off and was out the door the second they stopped moving, but seeing two entrances, one at each end of the building, he paused, unsure which way to go.

Sanders pointed him toward the farthest door. "The workers use this one, so it's usually unlocked, but let me go in first—I know the layout," he said, breaking into a jog.

Suppressing the urge to charge ahead, Colin slowed his pace and fell in behind.

*   *   *   *   *

D.J. Ferguson

As Chen followed Mickey down the stairs, his mind worked furiously to come up with a plan. The only thing he could think of was to shove her from behind. She was already a few steps ahead, and he hurried to catch up, trying not to make any noise that would alert her. Sweat ran down the side of his face, and his breathing was shallow and strained. Almost within reach, Chen hesitated. What if the fall didn't hurt her? She was athletic and fit, not much smaller than he was, and he wouldn't get a second chance. But he had to do something, and he'd better do it soon.

Feeling the weight of the computer in his left hand, Chen focused on the back of Mickey's head as she took the stairs one at a time. He must get those glasses—there was no other way. Heart pounding like a jack hammer, he gripped the handle tightly with clammy fingers and brought his arm back, getting ready to swing.

Just as he started to make his move, Mickey reached the bottom of the stairs, stepped off to the side and turned to say something. Chen's arm went limp, and he almost lost his grip on the computer. He felt the blood rush to his face, and his knees trembled. Not trusting himself to speak, he swallowed and cleared his throat.

"Are you okay? You don't look so hot all of a sudden. Why don't you go ahead and lock up, and I'll just meet you outside," Mickey said, frowning.

"I…uh…think maybe I am coming down with flu. I feel little dizzy for a minute. It is nothing." Chen continued past Mickey without looking at her and headed for the door at the rear of the plant near the loading bay. A forklift was parked near the roll-up door, and off to the right were long rows of tables used for cracking and sorting, some with shallow bins for rinsing and soaking roe, and several stacks of empty totes.

Cursing himself for missing his chance on the stairs, Chen snapped the deadbolt into place and snuck a glance back at Mickey. She had wandered between the rows of tables and was now standing near the soaking bins. It looked as though she were waiting for him after all.

Stupid woman, she suspects nothing. With a renewed sense of confidence, he started back toward her.

*   *   *   *   *

Hoping he was right about the door being unlocked, Sanders reached for the handle and gave it a twist, relieved to feel it turn beneath his grip. Jerking the door open, he stepped inside with Colin right on his heels. The narrow room had metal lockers down one side and a long coat rack hung with rubber aprons on the opposite side. An open doorway led into the worker's lunch room with a long table in the center of the room, counter and sink against the wall, and a small refrigerator tucked in one corner.

A door to the right opened into a walk-through storage area, stocked with wooden uni trays, plastic mesh baskets, boxes of rubber gloves and cartons of alum.

The light behind them cast shadows on the concrete floor, and their shoes made a soft scuffing sound as they approached a closed door at the far end. As Sanders reached to open it, Colin heard the faint sound of voices and whispered urgently, "I think I heard someone just now. Let's go!"

*   *   *   *   *

"Last load of urchin look very good," Chen said, waving an arm toward the large walk-in cooler. "Maybe you like to see the finished product?"

"Give me a break," Mickey said. "I know the urchins were good—at least mine were–and I haven't forgotten how you guys tried to screw us on the price." She glared at him and shook her head. "No, I don't want to look at urchin roe. The only thing I want to do right now is help nail the son-of-a-bitch who killed George."

D.J. Ferguson

She turned and started down an aisle, headed for the exit. Chen followed a short distance behind, panic squeezing his throat as he looked ahead, trying to decide where to make his move. About four paces in front of Mickey, he spotted a tote filled with drainage water from one of the rinsing tables, and a faint smile formed on his lips. The water should have been dumped by the workers when they cleaned up, but fate had provided him with a stroke of good fortune. Tightening his grip on the computer case, he raised his voice to get Mickey's attention.

"Unbelievable! Look at this! Cannot trust workers to do good job. I must check everything myself."

Mickey looked down at the bronze-colored water spotted with bits of kelp and tiny pieces of roe and wrinkled her nose in distaste.

Chen was already moving. Using both hands, he swung the heavy case upward in a flashing arc as he rushed toward her. Mickey saw a blur of motion from the corner of her eye and had started to turn when the computer slammed the side of her head just above the ear. She was momentarily blinded by a brilliant flash of light inside her head, followed by sharp stabbing pain behind the eyes. Staggering sideways against the tote, she reached out for support, but missed the low edge, her hand plunging uselessly into the water.

Wasting no time, Chen swung again, connecting solidly with the back of her head, and Mickey collapsed limply against the side of the tote. Dropping the case, he boosted her over the edge of the tote into the water, grabbed a handful of hair and the collar of her jacket, and pushed her beneath the surface. She offered no resistance, but Chen wanted to make sure the bitch was finished before letting go.

The shock of the cold water brought Mickey around, and she tried to inhale, sucking in a mouthful of putrid water. Opening her eyes, she saw Chen's shadowy image looming above her and realized what was happening. Filled with panic, she flailed her arms, reaching for the surface, and felt his hand on her jacket. Mickey gouged his wrist with her nails and struggled to pry his fingers open, desperate for air. Kicking her feet against the side of the tote, she thrashed wildly, but couldn't break free.

Her lungs on fire, she fought the urge to breathe. Using her last bit of strength, she pried frantically at his fist and managed to get hold of his little finger. Bending it backwards with all her might, she felt the finger snap, and he jerked his hand away. But with his other hand still gripping her hair, Mickey was trapped beneath the surface, and she felt the darkness closing in.

*   *   *   *   *

"Noooo!" Colin's shout echoed through the building like a gunshot.

In the far corner of the plant, Chen looked up with a startled expression, his eyes widening in fear. For a split second, he was frozen in place. Turning suddenly, he let go of Mickey and sprinted toward the door.

Colin was already on the move, streaking between the rows of tables, and he focused on Chen, his eyes blazing with fury. Legs pumping, he swerved around the end of a table and caught sight of Mickey clinging weakly to the side of the tote. She coughed violently, gasping for breath, and Colin hesitated, wanting to make sure she was all right.

Sanders urged him on. "Don't stop! Go on! Get the bastard! I'll see to Mickey." Returning his attention to Chen, Colin saw him hit the exit door at half speed and reach for the deadbolt, fumbling to unlock it. Colin surged ahead, closing in fast. Chen glanced back over his shoulder, let out an anguished cry and jerked desperately at the handle. Pushing the door open, he slipped through and slammed it shut just as Colin got there.

Colin tried to slow himself, but there wasn't time. Putting his hands out to protect his face, he crashed into the metal door at full speed. The shock jarred his teeth and sent a jolt of fire up his arms, but he ignored the pain and grabbed for the handle.

Chen was already halfway across the gravel parking lot when Colin started after him. He had closed the gap to about thirty feet when Chen glanced back over his shoulder and saw him. Driven by panic, Chen put on a burst of speed, and Colin responded by pushing himself even harder. The bastard was not going to get away. Kicking up pieces of gravel, Colin gained on him, close enough now to see the sweat on the back of his shirt and hear his breath coming in loud, ragged gasps.

Only a few feet behind, Colin knew he had him. As Chen made a leap to clear the drainage ditch at the edge of the parking lot, Colin slammed him in the back with both hands and sent him sprawling face down in the tall, wet grass. Landing on top of Chen, he planted his knees in the small of his back, right above the kidneys. Chen screamed in agony and tried curling himself into a ball, but Colin grabbed him by the shoulder, rolled him over and straddled him.

"You son-of-a bitch, you're gonna pay," Colin hissed and punched him as hard as he could in the face. Pulling his fist back, he hit him again, breaking Chen's nose and drawing blood. Unable to stop himself, he launched a barrage of punches directly at Chen's head.

All of a sudden, Colin felt a bear-lock around his shoulders as he was yanked backwards, and a voice rasped harshly in his ear, "Sheriff's Officer—hold it right there."

"I'm not through with him," Colin growled, trying to break free. "The son-of-a-bitch tried to kill Mickey."

"Looks to me like you're the one doing the killing," the deputy said, holding Colin tightly until he felt him relax.

Slowly coming out of his rage, Colin focused his gaze on Chen's face. It was a swollen bloody mess, and his own hands were slippery with blood. Christ, he would've killed the guy. Feeling the deputy turn him loose, Colin got to his feet, his legs trembling unsteadily. Moaning loudly, Chen rolled over on his side and covered his face with his hands. Colin stared down at him for several seconds, filled with contempt, then turned and ran back toward the building to check on Mickey.

Chapter *Thirty-One*

*A*fter explaining to the Sheriff's deputies that Chen was suspected of murdering Kessler, and telling them about his attack on Mickey, Sanders put in a call to Holt. He filled him in on the latest events and was pleased to learn that Holt would be available to book Chen personally. Sanders returned to find Mickey sitting in the open doorway of the ambulance, a blanket draped around her shoulders. Relieved to see that her eyes were bright and focused, he squatted down beside her and asked how she felt.

"Besides being cold, wet, slightly beat-up and really pissed...I feel just fine."

Sanders allowed himself a little smile. "You're one tough lady, but you need to let them take you to the hospital and get checked out."

Mickey responded with a negative shake of her head and stared out across the parking area, watching as one of the deputies loaded Chen into the back of a Sheriff's car and slammed the door. She shivered beneath the blanket, recalling the feeling of total panic, knowing she was fighting for her life—and losing.

"Boy, I sure didn't see that coming," she said, exhaling forcefully. "Maybe I'm slow or something, but I still don't get it. Chen must have known about George's death, but why didn't he just turn those guys in? Why try and kill me?"

"Don't feel bad. I didn't see it coming either," Brad said, putting an arm around her. "It turns out that Chen is the one who murdered George."

"What? How did you figure that out? I didn't even know he was there."

"From questioning Bart. He told me that Chen must have been waiting somewhere close by while they unloaded the urchins because right afterwards, Drake went and collected their money. Chen probably didn't trust his driver with that much cash."

"God, what a fool I've been," Mickey said, shaking her head in disbelief. "There I was, asking Chen to help me find out who killed George, and it was him all along. I was so sure it was Drake—and Chen always seemed like such a wimp–the thought never even crossed my mind that he might be the killer. Christ, I feel like one of those dumb broads in the movies who go off on their own and get into trouble. So....stupid!"

Sanders smiled, his eyes twinkling with humor. "Don't be too hard on yourself. If it wasn't for you, Chen probably would've gotten away with it."

"What makes you say that?"

"Apparently, he was feeling the heat and had already decided to skip the country. Upstairs in his office, we found airline reservations for next Sunday. He'll be going away soon—but not to the Bahamas."

Mickey smiled, then gave him a thoughtful look. "I tried calling you earlier to tell you about the glasses, but couldn't get through. So how did you make the connection between the poaching and George's death? How did you put it all together?"

"It's been a busy morning. I didn't even know George had been murdered until Holt called me, wanting to know where those glasses were. He thought I knew what was going on and was upset that I hadn't informed him."

"But how did he find out?" Mickey asked, more confused than ever.

"I'd better let him answer that one himself," Sanders said, sidestepping tactfully. "But after he told me about the glasses, I went back and had another chat with Drake's tender. Bart finally admitted hearing a noise that could've been a boat, but he denied seeing George that night and insisted they were all right there together during the unloading. Then he dropped the bomb, said that after they finished, Steve went to collect their money from Chen."

"So, you went looking for me, and Colin told you that I was coming here to see Chen." Mickey took a deep breath and blew it out. "I have to say, I'm awfully glad you guys showed up when you did."

"Yeah, well, next time you decide to stir up a hornet's nest, take me with you," Colin said, smiling as he rounded the end of the ambulance.

"Hopefully, there won't be a next time—but if there is—you got yourself a deal," she said, nodding her head.

One of the paramedics interrupted her, saying, "Excuse me, ma'am, but we need to get you buckled in for the ride to the hospital. If you'll just move inside, we can get you ready to go."

Mickey pushed some loose strands of wet hair out of her face and stared at the young ambulance attendant, taking in the soft peach fuzz on his chin.

"I don't need to go to the hospital. There's nothing wrong with me."

"Ma'am, you suffered a severe blow to the head. We need to take you in for X-rays, and they may even want to keep you overnight."

Colin grinned, knowing how much she hated it when someone called her ma'am.

"Look, sonny boy, you're not the one who pays my bills, and I have no intention of paying for a ride in your over-priced meat wagon." She stood up, still clutching the blanket, and noticed Colin's grin. "What's so funny, Nimrod?"

Colin walked over and gave her a hug, and she squeezed him tightly around the waist, leaning her head against his chest.

"Would you please try to reason with her?" the attendant asked Colin.

"I'll try, but it won't do any good–for the same reason they probably won't find anything wrong with her—she's the most hard-headed woman I know." Mickey poked him in the side, and he laughed.

"Tell you what," Colin suggested. "How about this? I'll drive you over to emergency so they can check you out, and then we'll grab a bite to eat before heading back to Neah Bay."

"It isn't necessary. I'm fine. All I need is a stiff drink and a good night's sleep, and I'll be good as new. Just take me home."

"Listen," Colin said. "You may be the captain when we're out on the boat, but right now we're on solid ground, and you're going to the hospital, even if it means I have to throw you over my shoulder to get you there."

Mickey glared at him for several seconds before admitting defeat. "All right, sucker, but you're buying dinner."

Colin backed up and looked her over carefully. Her wet hair hung limply about her shoulders, and she had tiny pieces of kelp stuck to her face. "You've never looked better, babe," he said, grinning. "But maybe we'll just hit the drive-up window at McDonald's on our way out of town. They don't have a dress code."

Mickey looked down at her soggy jeans and smiled. "Thanks a lot. I'll take a rain-check. Next time we come to town, you're buying—and I get to pick the place."

Colin groaned dramatically, and Mickey, still hugging the blanket, headed for the truck.

EPILOGUE

*F*acing murder charges in the death of George Kessler, and assault charges, with intent to commit murder, on Mickey Sutter, Scott Chen was being held in the Clallam County Jail. He called his wife and desperately pleaded with her to post his bail, and she agreed, but only after he signed a power-of-attorney giving her total control of the business and all their bank accounts. The other stipulation was that he was not to return to their home or call her. She wanted nothing else to do with him. The day after he was released on bail, she filed for divorce. Crushed by the grim reality of his situation, Chen locked himself in his motel room and consumed a bottle of sleeping pills, washing them down with a pint of cheap Scotch. The maid found his body the next morning.

When Bart appeared before the judge on the poaching violation, Sanders kept his promise and put in a good word for him. Bart was ordered to pay a five-hundred dollar fine and sentenced to six months in jail, suspended on the condition that he receive no further violations during his two-year probation.

Convicted of poaching, Steve and Ted Drake were sentenced to a year in jail, ordered to pay a five thousand dollar fine, and permanently lost possession of *Intruder*. Their attorney immediately filed an appeal, but after hearing that the Drake brothers had vowed to get even with those who testified against them, the judge ruled that they would remain in custody during the appeal process.

During the Drake trial, Mickey and Colin were still diving at Neah Bay, and after hearing the verdict, Mickey slept better than she had in weeks. With higher than average prices, it turned out to be a profitable season, but they were both glad when it was time to pull the plug and head back home to Port Townsend.

ABOUT THE AUTHOR

Author photo by Laurie Bliss

D.J. Ferguson spent twenty years in the commercial diving and fishing business before launching a career in writing. Troubled Waters, the first novel in the Mickey Sutter mystery series, is based on her first-hand experience as a sea urchin diver, working along the coasts of California, Washington and Alaska.